"Like Denis Johnson, Lu[...] urgency that it can be pl[...] but the stories in *A Creature Wanting Form* are rendered with a lyricism that seems to be in awe of the world even as they describe its greatest pains and profound injustices. Unforgettable, original, and a more than worthy extension of the far-reaching and hard-won empathy which characterizes the brilliant Hell World."

—Megan Nolan, author of *Acts of Desperation*

"In these stories, Luke O'Neil yanks the heart out of the dying world and makes us give a fuck that it's still beating."

—Rax King, author of *Tacky: Love Letters to the Worst Culture We Have to Offer*

"If you don't hear the rhythms in Luke O'Neil's writing, has your brain even been broken by the internet? The poster's James Joyce."

—Spencer Ackerman, Pulitzer and National Magazine Award-winning journalist and author of *Reign of Terror: How The 9/11 Era Destabilized America and Produced Trump*

"Cunning and poetic revelations into the sick sad world we're all glued to, woven with alluringly tapestried parables Luke O'Neil then pulls out from under us, rug-like, in choreographed slow motion. I am trying to dissociate from truth over here, Luke, and there are almost no commas for me to hide behind in this book!"

—Sadie Dupuis of Speedy Ortiz & Sad13, author of *Cry Perfume*

"Luke O'Neil has made an art of staring into the void, meticulously cataloging its horrors, and then telling them all to fuck right off. His new book is a gorgeous, unsettling, infuriating collection of essays and stream-of-consciousness poems about the daily carnage of American life, the ugly lows and brief, glittering highs of scraping by as what passes for a normal person in this country. There really is no one else out there doing what he does, and we're lucky to have him (though good luck saying something as soft as that to his face)."

—Kim Kelly, author of *Fight Like Hell:*
The Untold History of American Labor

"Luke is one of the few writers who I'll read for the prose alone. In this collection he puts his formidable stylistic gifts to work in a book that captures the feeling of living in 21st-century America exceptionally well."

—Ryan Cooper, editor at *The American Prospect* and author
of *How Are You Going to Pay for That?*

"A lot of the stories in Luke O'Neil's collection are pretty fucking depressing, because they are about the world we live in and the world we're about to live in, but in each one there's always a bright moment of joy or a joke or a formal invention that really lights up my brain. So then I read the next one, because you've got to do something, right? Turns out the whole experience of reading the book is a metaphor for life! Shaking my damn head, I gotta hand it to Luke. He really got me good."

—Dan Kois, editor at *Slate* and author of *The World Only*
Spins Forward, and *How to Be a Family*

"Luke is scary. He makes us look at ourselves and examine our souls and think about what the fuck we are actually experiencing, as opposed to just idly sitting by as we all distract ourselves until death. I hate his writing sometimes because self-examination is agonizing and depressing. But it's also a beautiful disaster."

—Dave Wedge, *New York Times*–bestselling author and journalist

"I always wanted to know what goes on inside Luke's brain. Then I read this collection, and, well, be careful what you wish for."

—Dan Ozzi, author of *Sellout: The Major-Label Feeding Frenzy That Swept Punk, Emo, and Hardcore*

A Creature Wanting Form

A Creature Wanting Form

Fictions

LUKE O'NEIL

OR Books
New York · London

© 2023 Luke O'Neil

Published by OR Books, New York and London
Visit our website at www.orbooks.com

All rights information: rights@orbooks.com

"Atlantic" by Rainer Maria excerpted with permission from Rainer Maria.
"In Undertow" by Alvvays excerpted with permission from Bank Robber
Music and Rough Trade Publishing.
"The Flower Called Nowhere," written by Laetitia Sadier, excerpted with
permission from Domino Publishing Co. Ltd.

First printing 2023

Library of Congress Cataloging-in-Publication Data: A catalog record for this
book is available from the Library of Congress.
British Library Cataloging in Publication Data: A catalog record for this book
is available from the British Library.

Cover image: Johann Nussbiegel, "Vespertilio spectrum," after an illustration
by G. Dadelbeek from Johann Christian Daniel Schreber's *Animal Illustrations
after Nature*, or *Schreber's Fantastic Animals*, Erlangen, Germany, 1775. Image
courtesy Alamy.

Typeset by Lapiz Digital. Printed by BookMobile, USA, and CPI, UK.

paperback ISBN 978-1-68219-383-9 • ebook ISBN 978-1-68219-384-6

For Shirley and Bob Madden
and Maryann and Bobby O'Neil
and all my sisters
and for the War on Drugs who I listened to almost
exclusively while writing this
and for Maine and Massachusetts
and most importantly for Michelle.

We toss and turn,
in undertow.
Time to let go.

> —Alvvays, "In Undertow"

All the small boats on the water
aren't going anywhere.
Surely they must be loaded with more
than simple matter.

> —Stereolab, "The Flower
> Called Nowhere"

Maybe I've lost my faith in history,
and the only thing I believe in now
is the sound of the Atlantic.

> —Rainer Maria, "Atlantic"

Something is wrong with me but I think it's probably the same thing that's wrong with everyone so maybe it doesn't matter.

There's something in the water
a creature wanting form.
Our boiling sons and daughters
all writhe along the shore.

"Decline disaster impend
our thoughts now linger there."
Silver stirs an Angel
uncultured of despair.

The mournful pinioned raptors
profaning witching wind.
There's something in the water
waiting to begin.

Lonelier than captives
a jailor's jangling keys.
An incubating rapture
the bloody graveled knees.

Crushing rusted pistons
combust a dismal horn.
There's something in the water
impatient to be born.

A bachelor rag of horses
sprinting toward the waves.
A disinvested master
unworried who is saved.

The churning churning churning
the churn of churning churn.
There's something in the water
that knows it cannot burn.

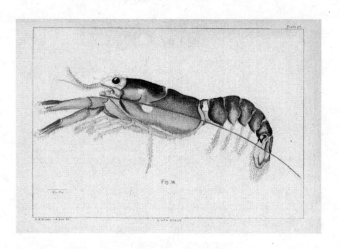

PLATE 23

Fig. 38.

Cape Porpoise

Do I look taller you asked and I said actually you sort of do are you wearing lifts or something and you said you had grown almost an inch recently which is weird because you're already tall and also forty-two and I am pretty sure people aren't supposed to get taller at that age.

The tide outside of the clam shack was as low as it gets and the air stank of its muck and frying oil and you said you were worried you might have some kind of cancer. The kind people who grow abnormally tall have you said. I said I never thought about cancer making someone grow you would normally think it makes them very small.

I always just took it as a given that I would be the first one to die among our group of friends so this news seemed like a betrayal of an unspoken contract we had all agreed to.

One of the guys joked that if it makes things bigger they hoped they got the cancer in their dick and we all laughed because penises are very funny to think about then everyone got quiet and went back to eating their fried fish meat and every time I looked away out toward where the water would be later on one of your kids swooped in like a seagull to steal a french fry off my plate and so I finally got up and raised my arms to the sky like they were terrible horned wings and roared like a dragon. I'm going to eat your bones for my supper I said and all the children squealed and ran around in circles as if it was the scariest thing they could ever imagine.

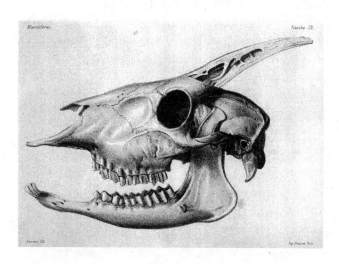

Predator mesh breach

There was a softball-sized hole in the fence of the flamingo enclosure and so the fox slipped through it thinking can you believe this shit? Doing Jim Face at the camera and wondering if it was some kind of trap. This is my exact thing he thought. The one single thing they famously don't want me to do.

The birds' wings had been clipped by the zoo and so there wasn't much they could do in terms of escaping now that flying away was off the table. That was basically their only move. So the fox got to work killing everyone with his teeth and claws and by the time he was done there were twenty-five dead flamingos. It must have looked like the hallway scene in *Oldboy* in there.

What were the logistics even? Did he take them out by the ankles first or what? Flamingos are pretty tall and a fox is maybe ten pounds at most. You would have hoped it wouldn't have been all that lopsided.

There was never any chance the fox was going to be able to eat that many of them in one go or maybe his entire life but when they all started panicking a switch must have flipped in his brain and his instincts took over and he went out there and played like Jordan in Game 6 against Utah.

The people at the zoo said it was the first predator mesh breach they'd had in decades. They said they'd inspected the fence just recently in fact.

You can imagine whoever was in charge the senior bird guy doing his rounds and coming across the carnage and going are you shitting me? They're gonna have my ass over this.

One of the zoo people said they saw the fox run off just as they showed up to the scene of the crime and they still haven't caught him.

The fox had killed one rare type of duck too on top of it all they said. The duck wasn't even supposed to be at work that day he was covering for his buddy. None of them were supposed to be there.

A really nice watercolor of an alligator

Apollonia said there were mice in my kitchen and she wasn't coming back over again until I took care of it and I said that was fair and she said to go get some traps at the hardware store and I was already planning on that but I didn't have any money set aside for it.

We'd been dating for nine months and my friends would still give me shit about her name sometimes like it was somehow my fault. My roommate Brad asked is it Greek or something and I said I don't know I guess her parents were big Prince fans and he said which prince and I said you don't have to be stupid all the time like that man. A guy called Brad can't exactly be the name arbiter.

She said the mice wouldn't be a problem if I wasn't allergic to cats which was supposed to be my fault too.

The next day I went to give some of my blood because I had more of it than I needed at the time but what I didn't have was forty dollars and someone told me that's what they would trade me for it. On the wall in the little room they have you go in someone had hung a really nice watercolor of an alligator and I wanted to tell the lady behind the sliding window I thought as much but she was busy doing her computer business. She probably walks by it every day and doesn't even notice it anymore at this point.

That's a nice watercolor of an alligator I said anyway just to sort of knock the sentence out of my brain and someone across the room under the TV they had playing said it's a crocodile actually and I said what's the difference and she told me that when a crocodile's mouth is shut the teeth still jut out just so and it looks like it's smiling like it knows something you don't.

One kind is from Florida I said. I know that much.

I asked if she had come here before and she didn't seem to think I meant it in the way it sounded which was fine even though I did kind of mean it that way and she said that she comes as much as they'll let her to get the forty dollars I mentioned earlier. Any port in a storm she said and I said what.

Then we sat there dicking around on our respective phones for a minute to reset the atmosphere back to neutral. I scrolled through the headlines and saw one that said water being distributed under police protection as crisis looms and one that said farm bankruptcies and loan delinquencies are rising and one that said Ariana Grande posted a video of her naturally curly hair in an iconic ponytail and another that said president just kidding about UFO evidence.

American blood is worth more the girl said. They can ship it all around the world because other countries don't let you sell it. They sell more of it than all the corn and soy in the country combined she said and I thought that can't be right and I started to doubt she knew what she was talking about when it came to crocodiles now too.

They have donation centers all on the American side of the border and people come from Mexico to make a few bucks off their blood because they can sell it as American blood that way she said and I said that's pretty fucked up and meant it.

On the TV they had a story about how many American soldiers had died since the war started which was 4,921. They didn't say the number for the other side. I think it was supposed to be considered poor sportsmanship to broadcast that.

They also said over 27,000 Americans had been wounded down there and they were going to have a general on next to talk about it but before that they called me in and so I gave a little nod to the crocodile lady and she smiled a little with her human teeth showing and then they took me out back.

On the way through I saw this one guy I know called Carl coming out of the bathroom with a cup of piss in his hand like he didn't know what to do with it like at a fancy party when you want to put your glass down and I said oh hey Carl and he said it's Karl actually and I said oh shit my bad Karl. Everything ok with the piss I said and he said so far it's pretty standard piss and I said oh good mine is too and then felt really dumb about saying that.

Next thing they had me sit in a little chair with a desk arm that folded up like when you were in school. There was a different watercolor on the wall in there that seemed like it was done by the same guy who I figured must be making a killing in the watercolor racket. This one was of a fox with a bird in its mouth running away from some hunters and the fox has a look on his face like oh shit and the bird has a look on his face like goddammit.

The lady with the needle asked me a bunch of questions mostly trying to figure out what kind of stuff I had done to my blood over the years and I didn't have anything remarkable to mention believe it or not so she was like alright that's just fine and she tied a blue elastic around my bicep and traced a gloved finger over one of my tattoos and said what does this mean and I said it's from some Irish book and she said yes but what does it mean? I said I honestly don't know I never could finish it.

Fail better she said and then the needle was biting into my arm and when she filled one vial she shook it like it was a little thing of tomato juice you get on an airplane and I said how does the blood come out it's like a vacuum or something and she said sort of like that and then it was over and she put a bandaid on and told me to take it easy for the rest of the day and I said you too like an idiot.

I took my blood money over to the hardware store and bought the mouse traps and on the way back there were some soldiers with their guns out poking around the trash bins and I had to stop for a second to think about whether or not I had fucked up somehow and one of them saw me and said hey are you from here and I said yeah and nodded over to my building and they seemed to think that was believable.

When I walked up the Caribbean lady downstairs was outside frolicking in the snow. I forgot to mention it's snowing. I thought she's a little old for that isn't she but then I thought maybe she's never seen snow before and then I worried about if that was some kind of racist shit for me to think.

I went inside to the kitchen and I saw a quick blur dart across the floor out from under the refrigerator to under the cabinets and I made a noise that I didn't recognize as something that would come from my own body so Brad came out and I said there was a mouse and he said was it the same one from before and I said how the hell would I know which mouse is which? I asked him if he thought it ever snowed in the Caribbean and he said no but he heard it snowed in Iraq once a couple years ago and I said that can't be true. He asked me what kind of traps I got and I said I don't know whatever they had and I showed him and he said oh no not the glue traps and I said what's wrong with that and he said I guess we'll find out and then we did.

The first trap I inspected the next morning looked empty but when I got closer I saw a tiny little mouse leg attached to the glue like the mouse must have chewed its own leg off to get away and I felt pretty shitty about that. The second one worked a little too well because it had three separate mice all piled on top of one another. The largest mouse had its face half submerged in the glue and one eye staring up at me like it knew me from before or something like we had had a disagreement which I guess we did now. The two smaller ones seemed like they must've gotten caught trying to help and Brad came over and gave me a look like see I told you and I said what are you the manager of killing mice? So what do I do now I said because they were all still alive and clearly having a very bad time of things in the glue there.

He said you have to kill them and I said how and he said smash their heads in but I didn't want to do that so I filled up the one big pasta pot we have with water from the bathtub and carried it outside with the mice in my other hand like a wilted bouquet and I saw the neighbor playing in the snow again this time with her son over there too and the soldiers were still poking around the bins and I thought that doesn't seem right and the boy came over and asked me what I was doing and I said I was setting them free so they didn't have to suffer anymore and I dropped the trap with the three mice into the water and a little steam came off their bodies and they sunk and it was over pretty quickly all things considered. I took out my phone to take a picture and thought about sending it to Apollonia so she would respect me and come over but then thought better of it.

I stood there with the boy real quiet for a few minutes and we watched a bird sort of struggling to gain purchase and slipping down the icy roof of the house next door where the lady who yells at her little dog all the time lives.

I said did you know all the roofs in this part of the world are slanted because that way the snow will slide off and not pile up and crush us all to death.

I don't ever know what to say to kids.

So I was like look that bird is gonna fall off the roof and it was all happening real slowly now but the bird wasn't actually in any danger at all because before it slid to the edge it simply flew up and away into the sky like a bird can very famously do and I was like oh right.

What does your tattoo mean the boy said.

PLATE II.

EXTERNAL MUSCLES OF THE HORSE.

Bones for running

A dragonfly bungled its way into the car as I was pulling into the parking lot at the new Market Basket up the road and I tried to backhand shwoop it out but it got itself turned around somehow and started ping-ponging between the dashboard and the windshield real fast like one of those videos you see now and again where the guy is twenty feet behind the table and still wailing winners across the net bink bonk bink bonk bink bonk bank. Both of the guys. Like missiles. Like dragonflies honestly. Look at this dumb idiot though. With its wings flapping so invisibly. How fast they go but useless now. A helicopter in a garage. Hundreds of millions of years of evolution only to be defeated by the sensible and safe affordable interior of a Toyota Corolla. This guy's ancestors had two foot wingspans and knew what dinosaur blood tasted like. I thought of our own great great grandfathers stepping out of the time portal at five foot eight with the vest on with the rustling watch chain and the high pants and their stinking dirty asses all spitting in god's face if they lived to sixty-five and here's us now sitting on our computer nineteen hours a day being allergic to milk and living to one hundred without even noticing that it's profane. I turned the defogger on high cool and hoped it would sort of wind-pulse him toward the open passenger window but despite having a head almost entirely made of eyes and being able to fly in a way that every evil scientist defense contractor alive is trying to replicate with robots he was totally chunking it. He was gonna die in the cranny there for nothing. In the nook. Just on account of how the wind blew him into my car. I was going to let it all play out off camera while I went inside to purchase the water and bread I need to make me alive but I felt bad so I went to gingerly nudge the guy onto my outstretched downturned hand so I could usher him back out into the sky world but he moved weird at the last second bink bonk bink and I put my finger through his little ancient skull and some of it ended up on the glass and the smudge stayed there for a good long while. All those scary little teeth accounting for scale of course and it came to nothing with respect to self-defense. It was like the bugs got together and put on a production of *The Opposite of Jurassic Park* where the people were the monsters. I guess they must have had their own version of Sam Neill and all of them on their side trying to save this guy and save the day for everyone but I wasn't aware of them as of yet and there was no way they were coming up behind me laying an elaborate trap. There was nothing that was ever going to get my ass as far as I knew. I was doing what came naturally. I thought maybe in the original movie the dinosaurs were just trying to help the humans go back to where they came from.

A conceivable tragedy

We had to wrangle the kids and have them sit down in the cafeteria while the guy with the big purple head folded his meaty forearms back and forth across his tactical beer gut and talked about how to neutralize an active shooter. The guy had gone to school here years ago and had spent some time in the desert as he told us more than once in the briefing beforehand. He called it a briefing not me. You could tell he was nervous about having to speak to children because he was sweating a lot. Or maybe he was just damp like that. He had been or was a gunnery sergeant he said and he said we could call him gunny but none of us did.

Sorry I got red-assed about this guy here but I was remembering a story I read a few years ago when people still cared about this kind of thing where a guy who looked just like this in my imagination talked about how our boys down there would send local kids into alleys to make sure they were safe. The alleys would sometimes be boobytrapped this guy said and so what they would do was they would take a bunch of candy bars or a soccer ball or whatever and toss it down the alley they were interested in walking down and then wait and see if any of the starving kids milling around would go run after it. If they didn't they knew how it was.

Sometimes they'd get an old guy and ask him to lead the way and if he didn't move exactly right it was the same thing.

So the guy goes to the kids our kids not the ones over there I mean he goes if a bad man comes in with a gun and then he was turning to us teachers with a look like we talked about this before back me up here man and your teacher runs at them then you kids should all run at him too and jump on him. Take whatever is nearby he said and he starts looking around the cafeteria and goes take a lunch tray or a chair maybe and hit the bad guy as hard as you can and then he mimicked how you would smash a chair over a bad guy's head. Down down down.

Most of my kids were all of eighty pounds.

No one has to be a victim the guy said and then he waited and said right and ten or twelve of the kids said right and maybe six of the teachers.

One of the kitchen staff poked her head out to see what the hell was going on out here and it seemed like she knew it was an alley she didn't need to walk down so she turned right back around. They were going to be serving Salisbury steak today and honestly it wasn't that bad.

After the assembly I asked my class what they thought of what the man had said and Luis raised his hand and said he would try his best to be brave but he gets very nervous when something scary happens and

I wanted to pick him up in my arms like Superman and fly him somewhere safe but I obviously didn't. I said we all get nervous sometimes Luis. Marcus was crying and trying to hide it but he was always crying so I didn't know what I was supposed to do there. Marcus was a fucking pain in my ass basically every day of my life but he was a good kid.

In the teacher's lounge later we were talking about the guy and the whole thing and then Linda said she heard that a seventh grader in Alabama or somewhere distant like that had brought a gun to school earlier today and killed three people so then I wasn't sure if going forward I was supposed to be scared for kids or scared of them.

I heard about that Jesse said but then they figured out they weren't talking about the same thing there had been another shooting like that a couple days ago.

I guess it was my job to die for these kids and I decided I would do it but I would really prefer to not have to if it were up to me.

I was having dinner alone on the couch later watching the weather and there was going to be some kind of big storm they said and then they said how many feet the water was going to rise. They had a reporter out by the storm wall with his big rain jacket on already and he seemed thrilled about the whole thing. I guess they must have waterproof microphones for these guys now.

We measure the damage of storms in feet and we measure mass shootings by the number of bodies but

I wondered if it would do anything if we measured shootings in feet too. If you gathered up all the spent bullet casings at a specific shooting how deep would they be? Or if you lined up all the bodies head to toe like you were laying railroad tracks how far would they reach?

I got out some paper and started scribbling.

The average adult in America is about 66 inches tall. Around 40,000 people die from gun violence here a year. 2,000 or so of them are children or teenagers so they won't be that tall but we're doing rough math here.

66 inches per body
x
40,000
=
2,640,000 inches

That's roughly 42 miles of bodies a year.

Does that seem like a lot or a little to you because I guess I was thinking it would be more than that but then again I've never thought about it in these terms before so I have no frame of reference.

It would take you about an hour to drive from the beginning of the bodies to the end depending on traffic. Your kids would get bored and rambunctious on the trip in the back of the car and you'd have to turn around and be like alright you two that's enough.

The average person would have a very hard time walking that far in one go. They'd have to make a lot of stops along the way and stay hydrated.

And that's before we even add in the 100,000 merely injured by guns per year.

Hmm ok think of it this way maybe instead. If 100 people die from gun violence a day that's around 6,600 inches which is 550 feet which is almost two football fields of bodies lined up head to toe every day. You couldn't sprint that far without getting winded. You couldn't sprint that far without falling down exhausted at the end gasping for air.

Common Grackle stoned to death by school children

Quiscalus quiscula versicolor

Boyd Elementary School, Fox Chapel, Pennsylvania, 1980

We flew together in large flocks whistling and chattering and squeaking to one another of news and of nothing at all over large fields of corn ignoring the motionless human sentries meant to frighten us. We followed behind churning plows and foraged through their bountiful wake for worms and insects and mice and near water we plucked leeches off the backs of turtles who stared at us dumbly. We nested in trees by the humans and ate from their scraps which were plenty and the braver among us stole right from under their noses sometimes as much for sport as for sustenance. For this we were considered a nuisance. Some of us would raid the nests of smaller birds and even attack and eat them which I believe now is the sin for which I have been punished.

Lying in the grass one day letting the ants crawl over me to rid my newly molted feathers of mites and biting lice a group of children approached and I thought little of it. These children with stone in their hands and stone in their eyes and stone in their hearts. Later the ants returned.

The Uninvited Guest parts 1 & 2

In the first painting the gentleman is tastefully appointed in a large black overcoat and a top hat. His head is dipped out of reverence for his solemn duties or perhaps to disguise himself as he pulls the chain outside of the apartment door to announce his presence.

He's in the process of removing his shoes before entering as a sign of respect and in the open window behind him the trees seem in first bloom.

Despite it all he appears to be smiling but it's rather the unavoidable showing of the teeth. It's impossible for a skeleton to frown.

They were staring at the little information card next to it like people do at museums as if it would divulge something that was being kept hidden from them in the artwork itself.

The artist inscribed "1844: Plusquamperfectum" along the bottom of the canvas which very roughly means more than enough time has transpired.

Neither of them knew that it meant that by any stretch of the imagination but that's what it meant roughly.

Is that Latin?

I think so.

What do you make of it she asked and he said I don't know it makes me think about the war.

When you say that type of thing no one wants to follow up you win a get out of talking free card for a bit but standing there before the painting more than anything he was thinking about how much longer it would be before they could go get lunch.

It was an anniversary of a day he didn't like to think about but his phone memories made him anyhow. It was a photo of a power plant or factory of some kind looming over the water of Buzzards Bay just at the top of Cape Cod. It's gray and raining in the photo and there's a bike path with brightly painted lines curving off out of frame as if to suggest infinity and when he took it the day they clumped some wet ashes onto the mossy rocks down there he thought it was this real emotionally evocative and moody tableau like it encapsulated Death Itself as a concept but in retrospect that didn't really track because the yellow arrows on the path are pointing both this way and that and that's not how dying or time works. Instead it all just goes in the one direction.

He often felt guilty because most of the stories he told about his father were about him either being sick or dying but for the past twenty years of his life that's pretty much all he ever saw him doing and in the first twenty they didn't have phones to offload memories onto for safekeeping.

He sometimes felt sheepish too because what a silly cliché it was to be a fully grown man and still be fucked up about your dead father but that's pretty much one of the main things men have to be fucked up about besides war so give him a break he thought. He didn't invent psychology.

It's very hard to spread a person's ashes without feeling as if you're doing it in an artful and mannered way. It feels too cinematic and performative even if you are only performing for an audience of ex-wives and conflicted children standing there in their gas station rain ponchos.

The night before in bed she had reread "The Sound of Her Wings" a comic book tale which was the first appearance of the personification of Death in the Sandman universe and is pretty much a perfect short story as far as she was concerned. In one part Death asks a violin-playing old man if he knows who she is and he goes No! Not yet! Please? and then a second later he's like Ah . . . well . . . and he accepts it like.

What can be done you know?

After that Death nestles a baby in a crib to her breast and the baby too is like Is that all there was? Is that all I get? and she says Yes I'm afraid so.

Later on in another issue Death talks to a different old guy and when they meet he asks her if he lived an especially long life and she goes You lived what anybody gets. You got a lifetime. No more. No less. You got a lifetime.

The whole idea of the series is about gods and their assorted colleagues who begin as dreams and then become manifest in the corporeal world the one the comic book humans inhabit and they remain real there as long as anyone believes in them and then someday when no one remembers them anymore they disappear forever which is basically what happens to all of us too give or take some of the grandeur and villainy.

She tried to get him to read it so they'd have a shared interest but he never read anything she or anyone asked him to.

I read enough when I was down there he'd say.

She'd talked to her mother earlier that day and she said she finally broke down and got hearing aids after years of her children asking her to. Her mother said she cried when she first put them in and she very easily understood why her mother would cry about that she wanted to cry about it too.

She grieved for her preemptively but she also thought it will be nice for all of the siblings to not have to repeat themselves three times whenever they tried to tell her anything.

Ma . . . Maaa!

In that disgusting accent she knew they all had.

For some reason he didn't understand he was trying to remember if he knew what his father's legs looked like. He knew he must have seen them on occasion at the lake in the stolen forest when they'd go camping but he couldn't picture them. He could picture his tattooed forearms however because he remembered stroking them gently as he was dying.

Years ago a thing people often used to say was how do you think those tattoos are going to look when you're old and he never paid attention to that but after all of the time in the hospital he knew now how they would look which was a profane joke. Not the inking of the tattoo itself but the decaying.

The next painting over was the second in the series. In it the dapper skeleton is jumping out of the window in a hurry and there are wine bottles bursting all over the walls as if the person inside the apartment was really going after his ass. It was funny like in old cartoons when the cartoon wife would get the broom or frying pan out and chase the cartoon husband around. The guy's little cartoon hat flying off.

It's not so much someone being gone that's the thing he thought and she was touching his arm and reading his mind now in the way a person who sincerely loves you can do. It's the having been made to watch people go so slowly.

This is why they invented the Irish Goodbye he thought.

Underneath the painting the artist had written "Perfectum" and then under that "Immerdar solche Vertheidiger" which roughly means always such defenders although that doesn't sound right.

Is that German?

I think so.

Neither of them knew this of course. It seems like it should mean never mind I gotta get out of here because the bone man looks like he's scared out of his mind. Like he's running for his life and he doesn't even have one to hold onto. It doesn't make any sense. What can the living possibly do to harm the dead besides forget them?

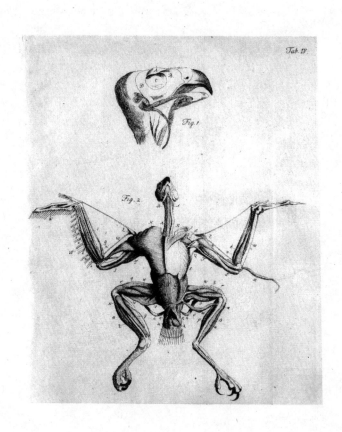

Tab. IV.

Fig. 1.

Fig. 2.

An international incident

There was a shooting yesterday that was one of the ones that was big enough that we all had to know it had happened so they sent me out to lower the flag to half-mast outside work. Half-staff they call it on land I don't know. I looked at my phone out of habit on the way back inside and there was another shooting going on. A real nasty one it looked like.

It wasn't immediately clear to me what the protocol here was supposed to be. If I were meant to put the flag all the way back up to reset things or lower it halfway down again still.

They had fired the main flag-knowing guy last month who had been in the National Guard a hundred years ago or something and this wasn't really my job in the first place but I said I'd do it so I wouldn't get fired myself.

I figured I'd be proactive so I lowered it down to the ground to one-third mast and went back inside feeling fine about it and none of my bosses seemed to care and then there was another shooting by the time I got to my desk.

I went back outside again and lowered it further still.

The next day I came in to work and you won't believe what happened.

Now we were in a Zeno's Paradox–type of a scenario vis-à-vis the flag height and its approach to the soil. People inside were debating what the definition of a mass shooting was and the managers were getting a little pissy about how work was being waylaid by all of us streaming the news on the computer all day. Trying to find out what kind of guy it was who killed everybody this time. Everyone hoping it was the other type of guy to balance it out. Like trading free throws at the end of a close game.

Being sort of new I was left to my own devices so I went out and lowered the flag halfway closer to the ground once more.

Probably not worth remarking on what happened by the time I came in the next morning and the next one too and just between us I was running out of real estate there height-wise with the flag so I went around back to the maintenance area to look for the custodian but there was some kid there instead who said in his cockney accent that the guy had been sacked so I borrowed a shovel from this kid he was an actual Victorian child with a sooty face smoking a cigar and everything and went back out to the flagpole and started digging to give the flag some breathing room so it would never have to touch the ground which was considered poor form in the flag community.

I had dug halfway to the molten core by the end of the next month but on the upside I was bulking up. The planet itself was spinning on this flag pole's axis now. I was going to hoist an upside-down American flag in a country on the other side of the globe at this rate. It was going to be a whole international incident. People were going to get shot over it.

If God should condemn us the way we do one another
Photorequestsfromsolitary.org

"So little moves inside here."

He asked us for photographs that illustrate the concept of movement.

"It's like living inside of a still life painting," he wrote.

"It's not living it's existing. I'd like to see things moving," he wrote.

"Perhaps traffic at night, lights shining and the trails from lights whizzing past. Or water flowing from a stream. A waterfall or snow while it is falling," he wrote in blue ink in a neat cursive hand that inched upward and to the right as if it were reaching toward something beyond the dark.

A slow unearthing

The kids had seen a video on YouTube when their dad wasn't paying attention. It was about the looming climate catastrophe and so they were shitting their pants over it. He tried to console them but he pretty much figured they were right to do so. He wanted to say you should shit your pants my beautiful little babies but it wasn't that many years ago he was doing everything he could to teach them to stop doing that. To shit right into the toilet instead.

He didn't want to lie to them but he also didn't know what to tell them that they could do to effect any kind of real change besides holing up in the treeline with a clear view of the executive parking lot at ExxonMobil and he didn't have the time to engineer some kind of *Hanna*-like child assassin character arc for them so he said why don't we volunteer to clean up trash off the side of the highway!

They seemed to think that was a fine idea and so he bought himself some time which is what everyone his age was doing in one way or another. Sort of punting on the whole thing.

Punting isn't so bad compared to a turnover.

Wait no that doesn't actually mean anything. You could convince yourself it did or of anything else if you wanted to though. Thinking whatever you want is free no matter how stupid it is. The stupid stuff costs you even less.

They lived a little far from an actual highway but there were reasonably significant roads that weaved in and out of the alternating marshes and farms and quaint little central greens with postcard-ready and newly-crowded churches everywhere and so they signed up with the town and got some official-looking yellow vests and the claw pickup tools he ordered via one-day shipping off Amazon. Whoops sorry he thought after. He got some trash bags and a shovel and they went down by this curvy stretch where the giant trucks carrying loads of produce have to slow down a bit that seemed safe enough a place to have his children labor in the heat.

For the most part the kids were enthusiastic about it all like they thought they were doing something real and every now and again they'd go daddy look at this and hold up a Dunkin's cup in their little robot crab hand and be proud about it. He was mostly excited about how little time they were spending on their phones.

Off to the side near some discarded energy drink cans he'd grabbed up he found a soft spot in the brush and he poked at it a bit until the soil and leaves started to give way like something had been buried there not too long ago.

A truck hauling lumber was bombing around the bend just then and he yelled hey fuck you pal in a voice that surprised him. With his full accent bursting through. He instinctually lunged after it as if he was going to chase it down. As if he was going to go fight a truck.

He was panting big gulps and out of breath with his tongue thickening and sensing things now and he looked back to see if the kids were watching and when they weren't he shoveled a few thin layers off his buried treasure and saw what looked like a jawbone and kept digging a little more against his better judgment.

There was the head of a dog of some kind in the dirt which he had accidentally fractured with his digging stabs. Most of the flesh of the snout had been eaten or rotted off by now but it was fresher than you'd want a dog corpse to be that you found in a shallow grave on the side of the road when you weren't expecting one. The ears were still there but the eye sockets were hollow and the lips were mostly gone and that made the dog look all jaw-forward and toothsome like a monster like something that was hiding just around the corner in a derelict spaceship and he shivered and tried to cover it back up before the kids saw what was going on but soon they were shrieking now too over there and behind him and over there and he hoped for a second that maybe whatever they were scared about had nothing to do with his situation. Maybe they were screaming about something they found in the dirt that was good.

Waltham, Massachusetts

Someone was frying meat in the kitchen attached to the waiting room and so it smelled like fried meat. I paged through an old issue of an old beauty magazine that was old enough that the people inside maybe weren't even beautiful anymore at this point and I sat there silently with six of you suffering in your own way and waiting to take your chances with a stint in the needling device.

I put down the magazine and scrolled through my phone and read a story about how the government is using dental exams to ascertain the real age of immigrants they apprehend at the border.

Someone in the professor's chamber was sobbing in a strange tempo. Their skin being punctured with the weight of a pianist's finger stabs.

One boy from Bangladesh said he was fourteen when they caught him with the drones and everything but they didn't believe him so they sent him for what he thought was a routine dental exam but instead what they did was check his teeth like you would if you were sizing up a race horse or like when you cut down a tree and open it up and dig around inside its tree meat to find out how many rings it has.

There are only two things most of us know for sure if we are lucky which are our birthdays and our names but we've long taken even those away from people who we decide don't deserve them. Even now we promote children into adults through the power of bureaucratic transubstantiation and that is because you can treat them worse after that. You just magically rob them of a few years of assumed innocence and then it's basically like whatever.

I didn't want it to but the frying meat was starting to make me hungry and then a crying woman was carried up the stairs into the room by her sons and it looked like her leg was in real bad shape sort of sideways and we all shut the fuck up as she tried to settle in and find a place to situate herself in the pain waiting room on the bad pain waiting room chairs and I thought it's strange how the presence of someone else in serious distress can make an already silent room more silent still as if coughing or even breathing out loud would be impolite to the person in question but also the concept of pain itself.

When real pain enters the room you have to respect it and hope you don't catch its eye like it's a bear you spot just off in the distance in the woods. So you don't make too much noise or any sudden movements and you back away very slowly.

Later you think you really pulled something off there and you tell the story about how you outsmarted a bear to your friends but you didn't it just wasn't interested in you at that particular juncture and will be circling back around shortly.

October 27, 2004

Across the street some kids were playing baseball which felt anachronistic in the first place and one of them socked a big dinger and they all moved instinctively and anxiously like they do when that sort of thing happens. I watched the ball arc up toward the moon which wasn't out yet but you could tell was waiting there just backstage rehearsing its lines and I thought people that young are walking on a tightrope they aren't even aware of yet. Not just unafraid of falling but oblivious to the existence of the chasm.

I was listening to *In the Aeroplane Over the Sea* I'm sorry I know and I thought that if you skip "[untitled]" you didn't earn "Two-Headed Boy Pt. 2" because in my day we suffered differently about things that didn't matter.

I never knew if it was meant to be I love you comma Jesus Christ or if it was supposed to be I love you Jesus Christ straight through no punctuation like was he addressing some person or the Son of God himself.

Jesus Christ I love you yes I do.

On my phone there was a grim dark storm cloud hovering over Rhode Island and the blackness looked like it had one little arm or flipper hanging down to do its damage with like a perverted little sky imp would have and there were two bright orange lights right in the center where the storm's face would be if storms had faces.

I think it was just the reflection of some tower lights though.

Next door the neighbor's dog was barking so sadly in a language I couldn't understand. Like when you're in another country and you need to find the hospital immediately or find your kidnapped wife and no one knows what you're trying to say.

It's good to be in those situations. Not the needing a hospital or having a kidnapped wife obviously but to be somewhere where you can't communicate.

To feel stupid and helpless like that from time to time.

To be elsewhere.

It was the anniversary of the first time the Red Sox had won the World Series after eighty-six years and people were remembering it all over the place. Someone on my phone had asked people to chime in with what they were doing that night and one guy said he remembered watching it at a friend's house and then calling his dear old nana who had loved the team her entire long life and had never gotten to see them win before then and she cried and her crying made him cry.

The funniest part the guy said was driving home after the game and seeing someone hopping a cemetery fence with a bottle of champagne.

Some kid thwacked a double and you could hear it so loud and clean. I almost spilled my drink. Some guy's kid and he's running around the bases now. Look at him running so fast away from God and the Devil and from everybody knowing instinctively where each foot needs to land without even thinking.

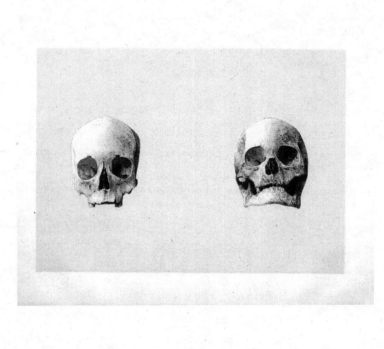

A loaf of bread

No one ever really knocks on our door so when someone does I assume something must be wrong like how it used to be getting a call in the middle of the night yet here was the neighbor presenting a fresh-baked loaf of bread she was holding in her hands like a loaf of bread.

I baked some bread for you guys she said and I said oh thank you.

There's a hornet nest on your porch she said and I said oh thank you.

It was 101 degrees in May and I wasn't sure why she was baking bread on this day of all days but that didn't stop me from eating it later when she wasn't looking.

When one of us would fumble the football in practice the coach would say don't hold it like a loaf of bread and none of us ever knew exactly what that meant. Coaches love to say stupid shit that doesn't mean anything but for the intensity with which they're saying it.

Hold onto it so tightly you don't care if you damage it I think was the point. Squeeze the shit out of it.

Unlike footballs loaves of bread are meant to be handled lovingly. Sticking out of the basket on your Parisian bicycle. Coaches hate Parisian bicycles and everything that whole thing sort of calls to mind. Maybe the striped shirts remind them of referees.

Hornets and other kinds of wasps construct their nests by chewing up wood in their little hornet beaks and turning it into a papery pulp whereas people chew on an entire loaf of bread and turn it into regret.

Some of the nests are underground but most are exposed like the sad one being built by one single hornet on my porch flying back and forth spitting his home onto my home one mouthful at a time.

Later I poked my head out the door and saw the hornet right around where I usually sit and thought ah there it is that must be the famous hornet I had heard about earlier.

When it gets cold a hornet colony will collapse but the queen squats inside hibernating alone waiting to start all over again later on.

Before that it all goes to complete shit though.

The first signs of winter drive all the hornets insane and they turn on one another and the young in particular and while they're busy fighting amongst themselves the maggots and the woodlice and centipedes and moths are waiting at the gates.

I just looked up hornets on Google and what people want to know about them is:

Are hornet nests dangerous?
How do you kill a hornet nest?
Should I leave a hornet nest alone?
Are hornets good for anything?

I thought that last one was kind of rude.

Then I clicked around and read that a wasp-waist is a women's fashion silhouette that you get by cinching everything together real tight with a girdle to accentuate the hips and breasts. Apparently at some point a guy decided he wanted to fuck wasps or at least women who look like them and then women had to go around like that.

I rode my bike over some altogether unrelated hornet nest far from here long before I knew how to hold the football one way or another.

Like other wasps hornets release a pheromone when threatened or when on the attack against prey in a sort of synergistic effect. So they all know it's time to fucking go.

Vespine is the term that applies to wasps. It comes from Latin and is basically the type of word a writer would use if they were trying to show off how sensitive to nature and language they are. Vulpine is another word like that. Vulpine means cunning like a fox more or less. How a fox might sneak into an aviary undetected.

The word synergy comes from the Greek term synergos which means to work together which the hornets promptly did that one time crawling up inside my chubby little boy camouflage jacket that I thought would have made me invisible to all of my enemies.

Around the same time the hornets got me but not the same day because that would have been a bit much the neighbor's dog bit me almost right on my dick and balls but it was a near miss. It was always a nice dog before that but I guess it had gotten old and was lashing out at its dog gods and its instincts were overriding its socialization.

I remember my grandfather becoming very angry out of nowhere like that at times toward the end of his whole deal which was scary because he was never cross with anyone. He hardly did anything at all as far as I knew besides sit there and tremble and let my grandmother yell at him for his quiet.

At the beginning of the end he was a janitor at the local high school and I remember hearing that the kids would goof on him because he was so slow and his hands shook so much. I want to go back and find those kids and shove hornets into their jackets. This kind man never hurt anyone even when everyone else around him was hurting each other.

A story my mom likes to tell me is about a time I found a dead mouse in the yard when I was a little pisspants and it was a whole thing for my brain like this existential crisis and I cried over the mouse like it was my dead son or something. They killed my boy.

I didn't even know this individual mouse previously. It was a stranger to me.

I think she likes to tell it because it reminds her of when I was sensitive and stupid instead of an asshole and stupid like I am now.

So I got the can of poison and I went out and looked at the nest and there was the one worker laboring hard and I pointed my awful weapon at him and briefly felt like a scab or a Pinkerton and then I noticed there was a large spider building a web in the general vicinity and I wondered which of them was waiting for the other to fuck up first. I wondered if they knew each other from around the neighborhood.

Another thing is adult wasps only eat flowers or whatever they don't eat bug meat but their babies do so they have to go out and sting a spider or a cricket or some other poor bastard in exactly the right bug nerve ending so it doesn't die instantly and then bring it back to the nest and lay an egg inside of it and then the larvae eat it very slowly and methodically piece by piece so it stays alive as long as possible.

Remember that scene from *The Road* where the main guy comes across the cannibal cellar and everyone is inside there still alive with their legs chopped off? Being shaved for meat like at the deli. That was just about one of the worst things I'd ever heard about. Nobody liked reading about that shit.

So I shot the hell out of the hornet with the poison and then I felt weird about not killing the spider too because who am I to play a capricious god and once you start killing it's easy to just keep going and the spider fell to earth and sort of just laid there in a spider ball huddled inward and the hornet took off and flew as far as he could go with as long as he had left.

Did you know a hornet can sting you just about as many times as it wants without dying unlike a bee who only gets the one shot?

When the hornets were attacking me I dumped off my bike and ran back to my mother and she told me to take the jacket off. Take the jacket off she yelled at me but I couldn't. I decided to roll around on the ground like I was on fire which I sort of was and thereby squishing all of the stingers into me. Stop drop and roll would have been one of the only things they taught kids about not dying at that point in history. Not getting into strange vans too I suppose. They didn't even teach kids how to hide from gunmen yet when I was young that wasn't invented yet.

The rolling didn't work naturally so I took off running to nowhere in particular but it didn't really matter because I was carrying them along inside with me wherever I went.

THE HYÆNA DOG. *Lycaon pictus*—BURCHELL.

A very long commute

How will we know if it makes it here you asked. On the wind like they say. However it comes. Will there be sirens you asked and I said I don't think we ever got those kinds of sirens built here. Infrastructure costs and so on. What about Maine I said. I'd like to be near the water when it happens. We poured most of my family into the ocean by the lighthouse there. You remember we went into the cafe. Yes I remember. What about my parents' house you said. I'd like to be with my own family again for a little while. I thought perhaps we could swim in the pool until we had to drink from it later. It was a hot and humid night and I looked toward the light outside the door where the moths had wallpapered the screen in their dusty agitated fluttering. Our tree is there you said. The one my mother planted from our wedding. It's got to be ten feet tall by now you said. Maybe we should get in the car now you said. I don't know if we'd make it there with the traffic I said. It's always terrible around this time of night even without you know. No I said. I don't think I'd like to spend another minute of my life sitting in that traffic. Commuting at a time like this seemed especially humiliating. I'd like to not be pissed off right now if I can help it. There's not enough time for that sort of thing. Being stuck over there by the gas tanks on the water honking my horn at some guy in front of me like what is his fucking problem.

But now I know what his problem is. Every single one of us has the same problem. I saw a cardinal there last time I visited you said. On our tree? Yes. Did they say anything about the birds did you hear? I don't know I'm sure they'll be fine I said. They have instincts about this sort of thing I think. Where to go. A radar of some kind. Tell me again about the tree. The bush I mean. It's a bush isn't it? It's a hydrangea you said. I bet it could grow forever if there's still rain later you said. I'd like to think I at least helped with that. The soil and everything. We could lay down under it when it's time you said. I wonder how big it could grow if there's no one there to tend to it. How big what now I said. A moth had gotten in and I was tracing its chaotic flight pattern. I was going to murder it if it was the last thing I ever did.

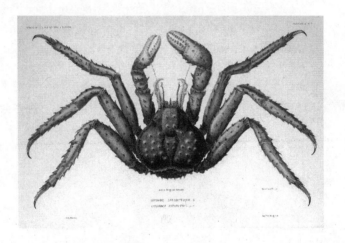

Proverbs

It was the annual fly-catching contest down at the fairgrounds and she was feeling pretty good about her chances to win again after perfecting her proprietary batch of vinegars over the past few months.

Everyone was settling in at the folding tables and chatting amiably until Doug walked in carrying what looked like a big jar of honey. Oh fuck you Doug someone behind her yelled. She didn't even stay to the end to hear them announce the results.

The ocean was crashing into everything

High tide on a Wednesday four perfectly symmetrical red pylons emerged out of nowhere off the coast about 300 yards out. Maybe pylon isn't the word. Like a big chugging ship's funnels where the boiler steam and engine exhaust come out. Whatever those are called. It looked like a ship was frozen in place down there just under the water I mean. Maybe four or five stories tall each of them. A couple of local surfers who saw its emanating paddled out to get a closer look and afterwards their other buddy said they never came back even though the waves weren't very high all things considered and besides they had been to Portugal. He swore he told them not to do it.

The cops came and arrested the buddy then roped off the beach and they sent some cop divers out to try to find these dudes and the divers didn't come up either and it was like uh oh so the cops arrested the diver's boss next. After that the soldiers came and pushed the cops back and roped off what the cops had roped off with a scarier type of rope. This was on account of the former president's compound was just up around the bend of the coast I would have to imagine. Also the uncanny nature of it all in the first place.

I wouldn't have known about any of it so soon if I hadn't been at work at the hotel on the cliff overlooking the water. Soon after the guests started ringing down for things they didn't need as an excuse to ask me if I had heard anything new and had I heard this or that rumor and it was the same thing every time I said no sir or no ma'am and then asked if they wanted me to open the champagne bottle or leave it on ice or whatever it was and then I'd wait for a tip and usually I didn't get one until I got a really big one from a sweaty looking guy pacing around his suite in a suit he'd never change out of and that kind of made me nervous. I'd been that nervous and sweaty before in a hotel room but in a much cheaper suit.

I brought the $500 down to the bar hot in my pocket and showed the bartender the $200 the guy gave me and she was like wow and I gave her her tip-out. Before I was a guy without $200–$500 and now I was not. I was gonna ask her to have a drink when we got off later at the other hotel around the coast and pay for it but I didn't. I would later. I would definitely ask her later. Nothing I could conceive of would stop me from doing that I'll tell you plainly.

I looked out over the front patio where a handful of guests were seated on the Adirondack chairs drinking more than usual and I had this embarrassing feeling like when you were a kid and you'd see your teacher at the grocery store buying cereal and it all of a sudden occurred to you for the first time that things happened in the world when you weren't looking.

On the TV in the bar there was a big college football game one of the guests had made us put on and they had one of those robot dogs prancing around and doing shtick like a little asshole on the field at halftime and the cheerleaders were all dancing behind it waving black and gold pom poms and the band was playing a jaunty rendition of "Jungle Boogie" and everyone was having a grand old time including the robot.

I wondered if someday they'll stop having the troops schlep down onto the field to march about and wave giant flags and just station a newer bigger robot in the corner of the endzone and it will serve the same purpose for the fans implications-wise.

There was a commercial for a new cute little droid Amazon was rolling out and I felt a visceral disgust looking at its dumb face like I wanted to kick the thing sixty yards through the uprights. Everyone cheering for me. Bill Belichick and all of them shaking my hand.

I never used to understand in dystopian stories why people seemed to be racist against robots very early on in the narrative like before they had even switched to being evil but then I realized that in their fictional world they probably had some odious billionaire that everybody had long already hated for exploiting them by the time he invented the robots so then I got it. It's humiliating enough just being ambiently enslaved by these guys I can only imagine what it feels like when the transaction becomes literal.

Now there were all kinds of news helicopters loitering in the vicinity and then a more muscular helicopter bullied its way over into the proximate sky from the base not far from here and the rest all sort of scattered out of the way like tiny little fish when a bigger fish swims through and this one dipped its nose down and hovered just over the pylons not getting too close mind you and it made me think of an owl in the low sky sizing up a sickly coyote calculating whether or not it could pull it off. Hungry and scared at once like that.

Whatever the bartender's name was which I may have mentioned earlier I forget now was looking at the TV and laughing like a cartoon witch because the robot dog had run onto the field run on to the field run unto the field during the game and some guys from the robot company were chasing it around with their tablets out trying to turn it off like clumsy nerds and they did look pretty funny to be fair. One of the players went to kick the thing and it stopped faster than anything has ever stopped and turned and reared up at him and the kid was like fuck this and ran to the sideline pissing himself I'd assume then there was a hammering that I thought must have been the boys in the kitchen out back tenderizing meat maybe but we didn't do that kind of preparation. It was like chunk-ah chunk-ah like someone getting his ass kicked rhythmically or like a tenacious boxer punching a side of beef hung on an ice hook and I looked out at the water and the helicopter was unspooling its gun at the red pylons or monuments I forget what they were called.

chunk-ah chunk-ah
chunk-ah chunk-ah

I'd like to say it was a last resort kind of option for the army guys but it was pretty early on in this whole thing to be honest.

chunk-ah chunk-ah
chunk-ah chunk-ah
chunk-ah chunk-ah

They were shooting and nothing was really happening and I've seen enough movies to know that wasn't a harbinger of anything good so to speak and next I was loosening my tie and walking fast out of the front door and then there was a sickening thud just behind me and it was the guy in the suit who had gone out the third floor window and he landed with his neck caught on the finials of the wrought iron fence and I shuddered and almost puked like a normal person would do in that situation but then kept walking thinking that none of this was my problem. Even then not wanting to upset the guests. But not help them either.

I wondered how much cash he must've had in this pocket.

Down on the beach there was a crowd fluttering and I went over to the edge of the cliff to look and a dolphin had washed up on shore and a dozen or so people were buzzing around it like flies and also there were the actual flies buzzing now around me like flies. One guy mounted the dolphin from behind and pretended to fuck it in the ass as a joke and I thought that was probably illegal but I also knew that dolphins shouldn't be anywhere near this part of the world naturally speaking so maybe it was a freebie.

I was walking to the parking lot they let us use a mile or so down the road and along the way there are all sorts of benches and pretty little spots you can stop to look out at the ocean and when I felt like I was far enough gone that no one could see me from work my old work my former job I sat down to pretty much shit myself and stared out at it all like a dumb tourist but not towards the monuments in the other direction. I knew better than that somehow. Like looking back was a submission to something.

I'm not sure if being able to look at the water with my mouth hanging open for any length of time means I'm an easily impressed dope or if we all aren't anywhere near sufficiently impressed enough with the ocean when we look at it. It could kill us all but it's so gray and pretty. It will kill us all eventually. The ocean is like . . . a pretty girl. I don't know man I don't know how to say that type of thing. The ocean is like . . . the girl from the bar I look at when I want to be alive. Whatever her name is or was. I should've gone back for Jessica if that was her name I thought just then but I was too much of a coward to do anything about her even without all the what have you transpiring so odds are I wouldn't now.

They had put up a plaque near where I was sitting and usually what people did was toss coins at it to make a wish to the old president like he was a genie or a saint or a wizard and I looked over to the east or west where he used to be alive more reliably and the only thing I could think of to do was to take a piss on the big stupid plaque as like one last fuck you like how an animal or a human soils itself when it sickens and dies but then I noticed there was a father meandering around just over there with his two kids in a daze probably thinking about how much he wished the old president was still around to handle all of this like he had with all those other threats and I figured I had better not have my nude penis out around people in public even now. They probably have a sniper across the water at the big house waiting for just such an opportunity and he would've sniped my penis clean off knowing these guys. Probably they were busy pointing their guns elsewhere at the moment but better not to risk my penis over it. I might need it later depending on the pylon situation.

Just then a stampede of squirrels and chipmunks and rabbits and horses which was a surprise to me because I'd never seen a horse around here in my five years came exploding out of the trees and into unto onto the dune brush and down the steep decline and with them the seagrass was soon on fire with the friction and then came the laggard mice and rats and some stray dogs who were too dumb to know what to do.

They were having a blast these dogs. Just to be around everyone. Smelling everything and so dumb and unafraid. Digging big holes for nothing. Looking around for approval that wasn't forthcoming. I envied them for a moment. I wished that that were me and later it was more or less.

The horses reached the water first obviously and I thought where did these horses come from seriously where and they plunged into the surf with a big chunk of elegant wet muscle and then all the other pathetically slow animals caught up to them including the dad and his kids and they all hurled themselves into the water too one after the other and I hated their slowness. Their heartbreaking slowness. I thought of a diminished crowd cheering for the last person to finish a city marathon. The condescending applause. How their sloth sickens you. How you want to throttle them behind the clapping.

The animals were crashing into the ocean and the helicopters were crashing into the ocean after that and their propellers were rotating underwater upside down churning and churning and then the hotel was crashing into the ocean and then the ocean was crashing into everything and I was floating toward the monuments and I would never stop floating for as long as I lived.

Altogether elsewhere some heroic guy was figuring out what to do and saving everyone else. Jessica too.

That was one of the last normal things I thought and I sincerely believed it. Now I had to figure out how to drown him and everyone he knew.

Maybe an hour into my roiling I couldn't tell anymore how long things took the last of the laggard unburned turtles waddled toward the shore and burrowed with all their might under the sand digging for their lives.

Summer.   Varying Hare (*Lepus americanus phæonotus*).   Winter.

The oldest gorilla in the world

Sixty-five years young haha there she was Fatou the famously old gorilla eating her birthday cake! They had spelled out her age in berries and placed it there in her habitat on a bed of leaves and when she ambled over she grasped it by the edge like a frisbee then laid down next to it while all the photographers and zookeepers in their shorts and everyone else stood by and watched. Laying down and eating cake at a ripe old age now that's the dream right there we were all thinking haha! She picked the berries off first then dug into the cake licking her thick gorilla fingers very deliberately all the while with a sort of aloof affect about the whole thing. To be fair she was German so maybe that was just how she was culturally.

There was a flamingo that had been living there in the zoo since 1948 they said and the zoo itself had been there since 1844!

The zoo served the National Socialist regime unconditionally it said on their website and maybe it was the translation but that word unconditionally made me a little tense like why say it like that?

Then during the war it was almost completely destroyed. Only 91 of the roughly 4,000 animals living there at the time survived.

There was a documentary where they put a robot monkey in with a colony of langurs and when one of the mothers dropped it accidentally they all got nervous about it and gathered around to sort of mourn for the fake monkey baby they now thought was dead. They seemed to be consoling each other. Whenever someone dies you want to touch someone that you know to orient yourself as still alive. When you wake up in the middle of the night to go to the bathroom and need to reach out to find the wall. I don't know if they were actually grieving or if it was just the editing and the sad music they put underneath it that made me think so but after that I read about whether or not monkeys mourn the dead and the answer was . . . possibly.

I sort of thought they would've been able to tell by their sense of smell that it wasn't a real monkey. Maybe the researchers or whoever sprayed it with some kind of monkey perfume. It didn't say if they did that.

There was a big study from Japan a while back where they looked at primates over the decades and it said sometimes they would clean the bodies of the newly dead or stand watch over the body or carry them back to a more familiar place than where they had laid down forever. Some of the monkeys would exhibit signs of depression-like behavior after a death and stop eating and just become generally miserable and then sometimes die themselves.

Another time I tried to read a paper about whether or not animals are capable of killing themselves and the consensus as best as I could glean seemed to also be . . . possibly. There was plenty of anecdotal evidence like one time a mother bear that some guys were torturing to milk her bile for medicine freaked out and killed her cub and then smashed her own head into a wall until she was dead. It was like what you would do if you were a person being experimented on for that long and had a chance real quick to end it all when the guards weren't looking. But did the bear know all of this or did the bear just kind of flail around doing whatever?

How everything you do when you're that strong is violent.

Fatou is one of only a handful of animals that were born in the wild currently living in the zoo the German zoo guys there said so she was unique in that she did have those first couple of years out in the world. She saw more of the world than most of us ever will. For a brief time anyway. From the Congo to Marseille to Berlin. I've barely ever been outside of New England.

The people from the zoo said in fairness that Fatou's age wasn't exact but she arrived in Berlin in 1959 at around two years old as best they could tell. A drunken sailor had used her as payment to settle a bar tab in France they said and they sort of skipped over the next part but then she ended up in the zoo and has lived there ever since.

After a while she got too old and lost her standing in the group of zoo gorillas so they moved her in with another old lady gorilla named Gigi in a kind of *Golden Girls* situation but then Gigi died in 2010 so that was how that was. I don't know if Fatou remembers or ever thinks about Gigi anymore. No one knows how to know that.

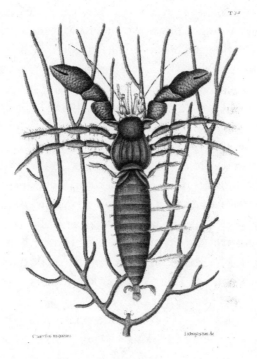

Caprella linearis   Lithophyton Ae

495

The reason for my stop is your brake lights the highway patrolman says to the woman. Yes sir she says and he asks to see her license and she chuckles in the nervous way you do when you get pulled over and you're trying to broadcast compliance which is the defense mechanism our species has adapted to protect ourselves from our only natural predator.

I just got a speeding ticket the other day I'm happy to show it to you she says haha and the cop goes haha no you're fine. He's so polite with her and it's just a routine brake light stop so there's no reason for anyone to think anything is amiss and then he walks back to his patrol car and returns and his hip gives out a little bit and he stumbles and he goes ah hell did you see that haha and she goes I've been at the hospital all day with my dad I know how it is haha and he goes I hope everything turns out ok with that and the thing is he says it with kindness like a normal person would say something to another normal person. As if he briefly remembered that he was a human being and not a spider.

It's like watching a fly caught in a web but it's worse than that the spider also has a gun.

Anything in the vehicle I need to be concerned about the spider asks her. Any bombs or hand grenades or rocket launchers he says haha.

He's killing it doing his crowd work here but he's a little nervous too you can tell. Like a middling skateboarder dropping into a pool is nervous but stoked at once.

There's a K-9 unit on the way but instead of going through all of that would she consent to a search of her car he says and she says ah well uh ok because she knows that she has nothing to hide and uh what harm could it do and so she goes to stand off to the side with another cop who has since arrived and it's like she's observing something happening to someone else and the spider starts searching her car with his eight arms moving so dexterously.

At first he hides the baggie just so but then thinks better of it and arranges it on top of a spoon he had ready in his sack and all the while he's shooting the shit back and forth with the woman and she goes if you find my missing scratch-off in there let me know and he goes haha I will!

His practice is paying off now he's done it so many times.

What was he even worried about a minute ago.

He's twirling and flipping through the sky defying the law of gravity.

Newburyport, Massachusetts

They drove north and east to go look at the ocean and then along the road over the salt marshes passing by the dilapidated but still striking pink house.

People are drawn to this house in part because of the story about its spiteful construction in the early 1900s. The tale goes that a rich man's wife insisted he build them an exact replica of the home they were currently living in but this time nearer the water and so he did without explaining that it would be in the middle of nowhere and set her up there before divorcing her and cleaning his hands of the whole mess.

The house has been slated for demolition numerous times over the years but local groups have regularly come to its aid hoping to save it. Nobody seems to be able to agree on exactly what to do with it though and so it sits there frozen in time taken over by wildlife and slowly giving way to entropy.

Some people just like it because it's pink and the way the setting sun reflects off of that pinkness and that's also fine.

The beach was chilly and the water was brackish and cold but not Massachusetts cold although he would have gone in either way because when you trek to the beach you go in the water that's just how things are done.

She always asked him not to swim out too far from where she could see even though it's what he was compelled to do. He felt unsettled this time and so he stayed close and bobbed near the shore waving back every now and again.

One has to be careful to not to do the I'm drowning wave. It's a different motion than the I'm still here wave.

She laughed at how his little head looked poking out of the water from a distance. A little fucking clown.

No it wasn't harsh like that.

What do you think about when you're floating out there she asked him later and he said I don't know mostly dumb stuff about our connection to the earth and things like that. The type of things you think when you are trying to not think about anything. Corny naturalistic transcendentalist Thoreau and Emerson type of shit. Man's powerlessness when confronted with the sheer awesome force of the tides and that sort of shit.

This time as he floated on his back he watched airplanes crisscross the horizon. Big ascending jets from Logan trailing lines of white cloud exhaust and low swooping propeller planes from the local grass runway. He was thinking about images from an airport across the world he saw earlier. Of desperate people clinging to the landing gear of a military plane as it attempted to take off. Of the video he watched of two little dots falling from the sky. People who had held on to the plane for as long as they could before they had to let go. Of the dozens or hundreds of people online trying to construct a bookending connection to those dying humans and the people who lept from the towers which he found somehow offensive as if a new horror like this needed an analogy to be registered emotionally.

He thought of a picture he saw of a military dog sitting in a seat on one of our evacuating planes and of the famous TV reporter and many others who squealed with glee about how cute the whole thing was. Look at this good doggy boy narrowly escaping the warzone with his doggy life.

On the other news they were trying to convince viewers to stop thinking of the people we had been killing over there as human at all.

When he got out of the water they walked along the shore a bit holding hands and knowing they were holding hands just to do it and saw a flurry of movement where the wet sand met the dry and they looked closer and there were thousands of insects of some kind being driven insane by the carcass and bones of a seagull.

What are those he said and she said I don't know I assume they are sea lice or something. She didn't know if sea lice was even the name of a thing that exists. If they weren't called sea lice already they should be.

Whatever they were they were scurrying in some kind of psychotic heat and the two of them felt a kind of shared visceral revulsion at the leaping maggot-like creatures and they tried to move around them assuming they were just concentrated by the site of the bones but as they walked along it turned out they stretched the length of the waterline for as far as it went.

Let's get the fuck out of here he said and she said alright and so they got the fuck out of there.

Some short time later on a different beach the tide was so low and the ocean was so far away and as they walked and walked she was delighted by all the hermit crabs dinking around in the wind blown rivulets and it made him love her like when they were young for a minute.

There must have been hundreds of them and they leaned down to get a closer look at one in particular because it seemed like it had a long silver tail reflecting bright off the sun but no it was just some kind of mackerel or something it had hanging out of its crab mouth. It was way too large for a hermit crab to have taken a bite of and maybe it was the hangover from the night before or the realization that everything is about to be fucked again from the sickness but the same disquiet from the earlier beach day returned.

The gulls were screaming in their horrible bird tongue like they were supremely pissed off about something like when you want to explain how you feel to someone so badly but instead you lash out and later feel poorly about it.

Nearby one of them was rhythmically jackhammering its bird nose into the ground so aggressively like you would if you were trying to break your head open against a wall if you were in solitary confinement.

It erupted from its sandy effort with a crab of its own in its bird mouth and the crab was also too big for the bird and then horse flies were eating the humans even though they were too big for them.

Sometimes hermit crabs will get into fights with each other. If an aggressive one covets another one's shell he'll go and bang on it and now the other guy has to come out and crab wrestle and whoever wins gets to take the nicer crab house.

A lady walking alone came up to them and said do you know if the water comes all the way up to here and covers all of this and being an expert on the area in the way you are when you've been on vacation in a spot for one day longer than someone else he explained that it did and in fact it should be over our heads right here in a few hours.

That night they crawled into bed with red faces and he tried to read.

As a strong bird on pinions free,
Joyous, the amplest spaces heavenward cleaving

Whitman wrote that about the glory of a bird's flight but that exultant untethering from gravity didn't seem to accurately describe the condition of most of the birds he knew personally. The state of being a bird seemed to be the same as any other desperate animal. We are all constantly starving and we don't want to be starving anymore. The pain of hunger and its obvious antidote.

Kingston Street

I was telling Joe about a video I had seen earlier of an osprey hunting a fish. It was a magnificent and terrifying thing to behold I said. The type of thing you'd say holy shit about if you saw it transpiring in real life. I said holy shit anyway even though it was just there on the computer.

No one wants to hear about a video you looked at but it was either that or talk about the war and that was all any of us had talked about for weeks now and there are only so many variations on the theme of powerlessness. You mostly wanted to cry about it all but then it would just be the two of us sitting there crying.

The way it usually goes with these ospreys is they circle above bodies of water and they can spot a fish from up to 100 feet in the air I said and when they do see one they hover and hover then begin what looks like a headfirst dive bomb but at the last second before impact they adjust their bodies so that they're leading with their feet to complete the strike and next thing the fish is absolutely fucked.

In this particular instance the osprey was successful and it grabbed what looked like a pretty sizable fish.

I read the comments under the video and some people said it was a shark but then other people said it was a dogfish and then other people still said a dogfish is actually a type of shark fucking dumbass why don't you go kill yourself etc. You know how conversations go online.

So it has the fish now and this was a curious thing to me because I would have figured it would have flown off directly to its nest or a perch somewhere to begin eating it but instead it circled around and circled around over a beach where people were swimming and sunbathing in the reddening shadows oblivious to the drama overhead. You would assume the shark or whatever would be dead or close to it at this point but then you see it wriggling around like it's still alive and I got the idea and I know that I am anthropomorphizing things here that the bird was giving the fish something like a tour in its final gasping minutes of a world that it had never had cause to know existed. A serial killer with a sense of sadistic showmanship. This fish that had never even seen land was perhaps beholding albeit briefly the entirety of the sky. I thought there could be worse ways to go all things considered.

I thought of fish Jodie Foster struck dumb with awe thinking they should've sent a fish poet.

That reminds me of when we were down on the shore last year Joe said. Where we go there are ospreys everywhere. We found a dead fish on our dock that had clearly been dropped from a great height. My daughter said that this was actually good for this particular fish because at least the fish got a sense of what it was like to be up high.

The Steve Earle song about the salmon and the eagle too he said.

I don't know that one I said.

I can't believe all these animals we have are real and we just take it for granted I said before drinking half of my glass. Growing up our parents tell us there's no such thing as monsters so we'll go to sleep but a bear is a monster and a moose is a monster and a bird is a monster too. Every bird in the world would rip your head off if it were somewhat larger and you were somewhat slower.

Imagine if whales didn't exist and then one showed up out of nowhere? We'd never stop talking about it Joe said. We would never get over it.

It's probably no coincidence that the most famous novel ever written was about how fucked up a guy got after knowing about one particularly angry whale.

It's just that we get used to the things that are scary Joe said. The real action is in novelty.

On the TV they were showing some buildings that had been bombed but it was hard to know if they were different than the ones they showed yesterday. You could tell all the reporters were very excited about getting to cover their own war because they got to put on the little helmet and vest and they love that shit more than anything.

Did you ever read that book *On the Beach* I asked.

The bartender was looking over sizing up our glasses and I gave one of those head nods that is only

88

perceptible to a server's heightened senses. How a fly knows you're about to move to kill it before you try.

People had been talking about the idea of nuclear war lately so I took that book out to poke through it here and there this morning. It's set in the 1950s and it's about an American submarine officer and a group of people he meets while stationed in Australia after war has broken out across the globe and they are waiting for the fallout to reach them.

They get to live a little while longer than everybody else does.

So the guy Dwight Towers befriends this woman named Moira Davidson who reacts to the knowledge of impending doom at first by drinking heavily and despairing I said.

Joe said I can relate to that that's how I spend most of my time and it's not even the end of the world yet haha and I laughed but only a little.

This guy tries to keep his shit together for the most part even though he knows his family back in the States are likely dead by now. At one point the two are discussing how the winds will eventually carry the radiation southward toward Australia. If they had blown more directly they would all be dead by now he tells her early in the book.

"I wish we were," she tells him. "It's like waiting to be hung."

"Maybe it is," he says. "Or maybe it's a period of grace."

I suppose those are the two ways you can look at a normal life in general as well. We're all born waiting to be hung and we can either despair over that fact or consider the interim a gift. Every day a last-minute reprieve from the governor.

Then we were quiet for a while after that.

What is a fucking whale?

Fuck if I know.

We live inside of a sci-fi universe we're just bored by its tropes Joe said. He was clever like that. He was a good kid but a real piece of shit which is one of the nicest things one guy from the south shore can say about another guy from the south shore.

Maybe that's why we have to fight each other all the time. To move the plot along.

There's a common thing in sci-fi when humans first arrive on an alien planet after traveling an unfathomable distance where they slowly take their helmets off and realize they can breathe and there's all manner of majestic looking plants and rock formations around them and sometimes waterfalls and so on. Some kind of space bird flies overhead and cries out. A tree that is much bigger than you would expect a tree to be. Sometimes the terrain is harsh and desolate and they're like ah fuck what now but they have nonetheless arrived somewhere else. They are standing on another planet millions of miles away and they are alive.

I never understood why they don't all fall to their knees and weep every time. Every space movie should just be scenes of people crying in awe for ninety minutes.

Would you want to do that if you could Joe asked.

Go to another planet?

Maybe the world is ending or maybe you have an idea it is going to soon and someone tells you you could get on a ship and while there is no guarantee what will happen you have a very good chance of reaching another Earth-like planet. Of getting out and walking around for who knows how long. Maybe for the rest of your natural life.

Then again perhaps you'll be immediately snatched from the ground by a space pterodactyl and hoisted up into the sky screaming.

In those last terrifying seconds you might see the expanse of the new planet for miles around you toward the horizon blushing in a color you couldn't name and think my god this is beautiful.

Ok I think I'd do it I said finishing my beer then standing up to pop outside.

If only to at long last know for sure that this right here wasn't all there ever was.

The next round came just then. I made a motion like I was going to pay but Joe got to it first.

Wait though do they let me smoke on the spaceship?

Aquila capite albo
The White headed Eagle

D. Size of the Eagles head

The Blizzard of '78

Here was my aunt calling on the phone. She's a nurse at the part of the hospital where the babies happen I can't think of the word for it right now and so I asked her if they had any babies getting sick or anything like that down there like you see all over the place on the news nowadays and she said not yet although there was one mother who came in very ill just now and they weren't sure if she was going to make it or not and so then I had to carry that around with me for a while until I forgot about it later. Like when it snows but only just so much and you figure you don't have to bother shoveling it will just take care of itself.

The mother was very beautiful she said as if that made it worse and it did.

She told me that when she was young my grandmother had a pig for a pet and she used to be mortified that the kids on the school bus would see the pig walking around the yard digging through the bushes and all that however it is pigs stay busy all day and I thought about the kids all pushing up their noses at her doing the universally recognized pig face and calling her Miss Piggy and having a good laugh about that.

Kids aren't especially funny although when I was young my sister who is still the baby even though she has children of her own by now that are older than she will ever be in my memory used to tell me she had a joke for me and I'd say ok what is it and she'd say she could only whisper it to me so she'd come in close and look around conspiratorially and say poo poo and I always thought that was a pretty good one.

Then she'd lean back in and say here's another joke.

Someday decades from now you and I will no longer be especially close although we will still love each other in our own way.

I thought that was a pretty fucked up thing for a seven-year-old to say to a guy.

My grandmother was never especially beautiful in her day my aunt said as if that mattered and it did. She left that for each of us. That wanting.

So I told my aunt about a story I had just read where a group of scientists got the idea to see what would happen if they put a mirror in front of some common pigs. That's what a lot of science is just thinking up something dumb and observing it i.e. we kept a takeout salad and a banana in the ceiling of my dorm room for an entire year because it seemed like a funny thing to do. We all secretly hoped it would grow a beanstalk to the moon and instead it just kind of slumped into a foul grayness and eventually it stopped smelling like anything at all. It's probably still up there for all I know.

So the scientists took some baby pigs and showed them their own reflection and the pigs were captivated. They'd rub their little snouts on the glass and look at themselves from this or that angle like they were getting ready in the morning for work. Pigs don't have jobs though everyone knows that. Besides eating until they can be eaten which is a tough business to be in.

After a while the pigs came to understand the correlation between their own movements and the movements of the pig in the mirror and so now what they all did there was they put a bowl of food somewhere that could only be seen from the vantage of the reflection in the mirror and sure enough the pigs figured out how to find where it was pretty quickly. It suggested that they have a type of self-awareness and that was pretty exciting. You'd have to hope they don't have too much self-awareness though. The implications of that.

The scientists also said pigs have very similar hearts to humans and similar teeth too. And then in the newspaper one of the scientists said that once pigs learn something like the mirror gag it's difficult for them to unlearn it. It imprints on their brain they said. Like sometimes they get scared and never forget the place where they got scared. They know in their pig hearts to avoid that area.

Then I asked my aunt if she had had all that many babies die on her at work there over the years and she said yes from time to time it happens and I asked her what that was like for a person to go through and she said it's like when it snows so much no matter how hard you ever tried to shovel you would never be able to dig out from under it.

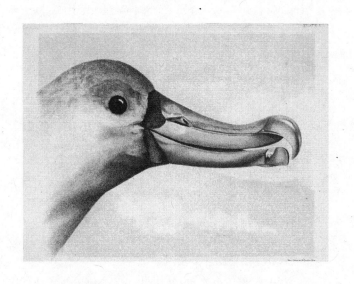
PLATE I.

Cape Elizabeth

Oh my god.

Oh my god.

Oh my god he bit me.

It went on like so for a minute or two building to the crescendo where the counter-melodies of the lines started to overlap through the muffle of Jane's earbuds.

Oh god.

He bit me god.

My god bit me.

It didn't even break the skin Jane murmured under her breath.

What did you just say to me Emily barked still eating now with pieces of sandwich spraying out of her mouth.

Jane pretended she didn't hear her. She thought her mother was a coward and a bully which is a sad thing for a child to think about their mother even if it's true.

All day Jane had been a drowsy rotisserie chicken on a sandy blanket not yet ready to admit she was invested in her family's melodrama. To acknowledge a parent's suffering with empathy whatever it happened to be about was to admit that they were a human being with their own distinct interiority. It would be a few more years into her twenties before that came to pass. The period when young people try to make up for precious lost time by befriending their parents anew.

Wait dad smokes weed haha ok!

Oh you're fine Emily's own mother in the ergonomic beach chair said pulling rank now in terms of suffering seniority.

How difficult it had been for her to ensure that all of these pale humans strewn along the beach came to exist in the first place never mind the surviving this long on top of it. And with no help at all she often said. This was due to martyrdom and victimhood running concurrently for generations on the maternal branch of her family. Alcoholism and invisibility on the men's side.

These birds are clever little sons of bitches she said. You've gotta be sneaky while you're eating.

I know how to handle these birds she said.

Her name was . . . Shirley probably. No younger than that. Debbie.

She'll be back Jane said tracing the bird's centrifugal swooping into the blue and pink and red afternoon sky but no one listened to her either. Maybe she didn't say it she just thought it she couldn't be sure.

There were so many birds in the tangible horizon over Sheep's Island you could lose track of a specific one very easily. Like trying to track a commuter at Downtown Crossing at rush hour. Even one who had just bit your mother could get lost in the crush.

Oh oh oh here it comes again oh oh Emily said but then the gull just strafed by like it was shot from a fully drawn bow and headed over the dune and was gone out of sight which meant off to the limbo where things you can't see right now live. Where mothers idle when they hold their hands in front of their faces to the baby's dumb horror. Where Debbie hid from Emily and Emily hid from Jane.

Where the things you don't want to admit about yourself are compounding.

Where the nips of coconut rum you toss out of the car window end up.

You gotta hunch over like this while you're eating your sandwich Debbie said lecturing in high townie dudgeon now and lighting a Kent Ultra Light 100.

Debbie poked her cigarette arm out and with the other one pulled her towel down doing that thing where people drape a linen napkin over their head to eat the famously decadent bird dinner they show you on TV shows sometimes. To hide one's shame about being rich from god. Maybe the person god or more likely the bird god you would think.

Emily had more or less been doing a similar move to begin with but apparently the gull was familiar with that style of defense from putting in hours of practice.

Jane watched from under her giant Instagram hat which was a kind of umbrella that shielded her own face from god's burning beacon.

Calm yourself Ma Emily said.

Grandma . . . Jane said and lacked the conviction to complete the thought.

Grandma.

In her one ear Jane's favorite podcast was clumsily plagiarizing a blog post about an academic paper about an experiment where they had managed to revive the organs of a dog after it had died. Its heart and kidney and liver and all that garbage pumping with new cursed demon life. Not the brain though. Its dog brain was still gonzo. In the dog zone.

They're gonna figure out how to make people live forever just in time for us all to have to huddle in caves she thought.

Eating poison oysters from the one all-encompassing ocean.

Too late for her mother and grandmother she thought but she and the two doofuses down there by the water playing grabass will have to bleed at the spear tip of that. The triumphant history-erupting torture. If any of them are even numbered among the desperate dwindling winners.

Oh oh Jesus Mary and Joseph her mother said.

Someone was playing "Summertime" very loudly nearby on their speakers which Jane recognized because it was her great-grandmother's favorite song something her grandmother told her every time she was drunk which was regularly and also right now. It was a very pretty song she thought.

One of these mornings,
you're going to rise up singing.

Then you'll spread your wings,
and you'll take the sky.

Probably not! Still a pretty song though.

Next Debbie started complaining about her carpal tunnel out of nowhere. To change the subject maybe. I can barely pick up a bobby pin she said but she said she had some kind of gel she can rub on her wrist at night that she bought off of the TV.

Pain comes at night because your body isn't moving she said.

Motion is lotion she said.

Ewww Jane said.

What dear?

Nothing Grandma.

Maybe it's pain waiting until you let your guard down to strike Jane thought.

She didn't actually think that. That part is made up but she could have thought it.

Then the bird with the two-inch-long shark's teeth it had impossibly grown since the last time anyone saw it swooped back around into frame when everyone had mostly calmed down. And now here's this clever hungry fucker again.

It didn't attack just yet it floated there not moving such were the angles of the wind that its hovering and stabilization made it appear like it was motionless above everyone like a photo like a still life of a bird not progressing in any direction in the sky just right there and content in its stillness. Nonetheless it was telegraphing its strategy and Emily was Bluetooth-docking with it and she knew what it was preparing now and she reached for her holster infinitesimally inch by inch like a handsome sheriff in a standoff. Her brain had been empty of everything else but bird since the incident despite all the carrying on. A cartoon thought bubble had been inked over her head and it simply read "kill the bird." Doing physics equations now about approach velocity like an air traffic controller even though she had flunked algebra. She had no mother and no children she was a desperate earthbound creature in the sand defending herself against the feathery sky.

When the bird twitched weird she clocked its pitch windup and choked up on her stainless steel water bottle and in bullet time donked the fucking thing out of the low air and it pinged so sharp off its lowly dunce skull. Her swinging upwards plumped up a mist cloud of sand that dirtied everyone around and Jane sat up for the first time coughing.

Ma holy shit she said.

Don't swear Debbie said.

Ma . . . holy . . . crap she said.

Emily was so fast and confident doing it it was as if she walked to the plate on her first day being called up and made contact off a heater from Pedro.

Not a base hit obviously but contact.

Holy shit crap Jane said again.

Death was involved now so she was invested. Oh my god Emily was saying all over again. The same whole performance from earlier.

Debbie was shaking her head and going I told you so. See? I told you this was going to happen.

She hadn't said anything of the kind.

She was responding to a whole other conversation she had been having that no one else was privy to.

If your father was here etcetera she was saying. He wasn't there though he was nowhere.

In her heart mostly wishing her sister was still alive. Not for this but for everything.

The three of them hot-sand-foot-walked over to where the bird had landed ten feet or so from the thwacking near the dune brush line and its entire beak had been blown off and was already being carried off by a crab and the top of its skull had been peeled back like a half opened tuna can sitting in an oily sink and so the brain was fully exposed and quickly cooking in the sun like a microwave does to a brain. Jane looked closer and it was crawling with a type of broiling liquidy insect larva that made her gag then Debbie and Emily gagged in turn like how the chain of infectious slapstick puking goes on a sketch show.

What is that?

What the fuck is that?

Don't swear!

Shut the fuck up!

What did you say?

What is that?

Shut the fuck up!!

Go get your brothers Emily said to Jane establishing jurisdiction and it was either comply with that or stand there one single second more smelling all of the mess so she said fine and stomped down toward the water with her feet burning on the sand then not burning then burning to where the dumb shits were frolicking with their even stupider friends. A football arced toward her head and she punched it to the moon.

The bird's eyes were still open and flickering looking directly at Emily now narrowing and widening like playing with a video camera's focus. The brain bugs seemed uncanny in their movement like they were poorly done in digital effects like the movie they existed inside of didn't raise enough money.

Someone has to put it out of its misery Debbie said then presently jogged up the older lummox boy.

Whoa bad ass he said.

Kill it boy Debbie said and being too dumb to think about anything he got a beach chair and pushed the metal piping of the leg into the skull so hard half the bird was buried head down now with its ass to the sky.

Don't swear Debbie said and he said sorry grandma.

Jane meanwhile was trying to wrangle the younger one who was bent over in the shallow surf cupping up handfuls of wet sand and water and watching it sift through his fingers intently over and over. Like a little nerd she thought.

Come on back up buddy she said.

Mom killed a bird she said thinking that would jolt him awake and he looked back at her and smiled weird in a way that made her know her spine was inside of her. All thirty-three of the vertebrae lighting up one by one from bottom to top into her neck and to the base of her brain like a strongman hammer game at the carnival ding ding ding ding ding dong then hitting the bell at the top.

Look at this he said showing her a handful of mud.

That's super cool buddy but come on. We have to go help mom right now.

Put your finger in my mouth the boy said and she thought she misheard him.

Shut up come let's get on back up to mom. Grandma is being weird.

Put your finger in my mouth. I won't bite it off he said.

Ding ding ding ding ding ding.

I promise I won't bite your finger off if you put it in my mouth he said.

What are you talking about let's go she said and grabbed him by the shoulders and turned him around and when she let go she left bright handprints on his skin.

Put your finger in my mouth.

Ok forget it you weirdo she said and she went to trudge back up but the spot where the wet sand met the dry felt thicker and slower than it had a moment ago and her legs were heavy. Her legs were getting so skinny.

Stop joking around Michael she said whipping around for one last try and one of her earbuds tumbled into the near wet sand.

Michael picked it up and offered it up in his hand.

I'll stop if you put your finger in my mouth he said.

Which one she said.

Just do it. I won't bite your finger off I swear to god.

Which finger?

Just do it.

Which god?

A brief pocket of borrowed joy

An old friend I haven't seen in some years and certainly not since any of us learned the word Covid was visiting at the home of a second friend nearby. Come by he said and I said I would. There would be a pool involved.

Like everything in the past year or more any social or professional event the prospect of having to follow through on that promise instilled in me a sort of anxious dread which I'm sure many of you will be familiar with. It's not that I don't leave the house anymore I do in fact leave the house multiple times a day such as to go to the store or to the gym and then the store again later.

It's not that I don't want to see people I love and even people I merely like it's more that I don't want them to see me.

Not helping matters of late has been this persistent insomnia I've been dealing with. Not insomnia as such but rather a kind of waking sandwich. The falling asleep is easy and the drowsing in bed in the morning is easy it's the middle part that is the bulky protein of the thing.

Time to confront your regrets bitch.

I'd taken one of my bed stand sleeping pills too late into the night so it didn't kick in until I really did not need it anymore. It made my blood flow clumsily and my pupils were tiny pinholes the entire morning so I asked M. to drive us over scared that I would yank the car into a tree over nothing and then next thing

I knew there we had arrived and were floating in my nice friend's nice pool. I kept having to scoop handfuls of the water onto my face to wake myself up over and over like a chef's persistent basting.

I told my visiting friend who is the type of friend I can say weird shit to that I thought I had changed in the years since I'd seen him. That I was more nervous now and jittery about being anywhere and less confident and he said haha no that is how you always used to be before too and it was a bigger insight than any I've ever gotten in therapy. Oh right haha. Ok. Maybe I'm just who I am still.

To be fair I spent a lot of time around this friend high out of my mind so that could be a factor here.

Then I talked about actual therapy with him floating in the pool there my arm hair bleaching blonde in the sun and I said I had come to this realization talking of late that I was comfortable now at this later stage in my life in reverting to the sloppy Massachusetts townie I had started out as and was always meant to be. To strip away all pretense. All those years in the middle living between Boston and New York and playing in bands and writing for fancy magazines and such were an effort to overwrite my origins is what I learned about myself I said. For example how I had purposefully lost my Boston accent perhaps as a type of class traitorship I said and he laughed again and said wait you think you don't have a Boston accent?

I guess I thought I was getting away with something all those years.

I thought instead of paying a stranger to listen to us talk about our childhoods and our disappointments and fathers and so on once a week we should all have a roster of people who once knew us rotate into town to serve the same purpose. Only with a more solid origin base to work with.

It happening in a pool would be a nice bonus.

Maybe I just invented the concept of friendship.

To remind us who we are though. To fact-check the meandering stories. What does a therapist know about you really when you could sit there lying or embellishing and the entire session they're providing counseling to a person who might never have even existed. You can say anything you want after all. You could say you were a happy little boy thrilled to be alive and to be anywhere. You could say there was no singular figure in your life that you wanted desperately to not turn out like even though you did anyway. Were always going to.

Or you could tell her you were Batman who cares what does she know about you that didn't come from you?

I don't lie to my therapist to be clear but I could if I wanted to is the point.

Then I ducked under the water and swam away abruptly which is one of the advantages of socializing in a pool. You can't do that on land you can't just disappear and materialize some distance away. It's

110

generally considered rude to try that on land but in the water it's like oh he's just taking a little dip and then you float on the tube thing wherever the water takes you with your pool beer in hand unbothered by anything.

Someone's child I have no idea whose it was appeared with a ring toy and I gestured to her to throw it and try to land it on my head and she did and missed and we tried again and again until she got it and then we exalted in the victory and I swam away again. A brief pocket of borrowed joy. Enough of a small concentrated dose of adjunct parenthood to tide me over.

Now waded over a third friend this one who had actually known me as a child having by complete happenstance married into this group of wholly unrelated friends later in life and we talked and he asked me if I remembered his father's book store and how it had burned down or maybe how their house had burned down and I only sort of remembered either of those possibilities and then he told me about how all of their family photos were lost in the flames and how they held a party or a wake of sorts and everyone who knew them brought over photographs they had been holding onto of the family so that they could rebuild their collection of memories.

Then a group of people I'd known but only just so much and mostly late at night bobbed into frame and I thought I might try trading old war stories about partying and playing music with them but we talked instead about real estate the one thing that ties people of a certain age together. Good decisions we'd made and opportunities squandered and how certain neighborhoods we'd known intimately had changed over time some for the better and some for the worse and so were largely strange to us now but despite all of that still held onto enough of their original nucleus of identity to be worth remembering and to visit from time to time.

That one bar we used to all go to get fucked up at in Union Square is still there someone said. It made it through all of this. We could all go there tonight if we wanted to. We could go right now.

Kill Devil Hills

A crowd had gathered on the wind-blown sand waiting for the beach house to collapse. It was like when they dynamite the old football stadium but this implosion wasn't on purpose.

It was overcast and blustering and the seaweed-green paint of the house contrasted off the smooth slate gray of the sky behind it and after everyone had stood around like assholes for long enough the decisive wave came that toppled the thing for good. It was akin to a mercy. Not really but you know. So everyone could go home. The news guys with all their heavy cameras to load. After standing at the deathbed of a family member you were indifferent about for as long as seemed polite.

The wave took out its tall stilted beach house legs and the falling was slower than you would think it was going to be. A giraffe laying down to die but also fighting it. How it goes down on its front knees struggling for a few more minutes of oxygen and perception of the waking world while the guy standing nearby who killed it is taking photos and smiling and high-fiving his buddies and the local they hired is off to the side bargaining with his maker. Seeing if he can get a pass on this one.

So this house finally let go of the earth and was in the water and it got sucked out about 20 yards instantly on the inhale and started riding on the waves and this kind of surprised people because it just bobbed up and down for a while like nothing was weird. A whole house just about as far out there as your dumb kid would take his boogie board and go mom look at me mom and it was going up and down and up and down and not even near broken yet.

Soon enough the porch got dragged off into the sea but all in all it held together much longer than anyone would have predicted. They should hire whoever this architect was to build houses elsewhere. Houses that aren't literally within the stab radius of the water's tongue.

Someone said the house had been purchased for $400,000 not long ago which seemed cheap for a beach house. The views were admittedly very nice. A little general store down the way for milk and things. Muffins in the morning.

It was all going like that until one of the lower walls folded out like the wing of a plump goose someone's dog had ripped the shit out of. You felt bad about it all but there was nothing to be done now but for it all to go away. It was a house that became a houseboat for a little while which most houses never even get to do. They should've made all the houses we have into houseboats.

Why weren't we doing that?

Everyone was waiting for a guy to come along and build the ark. We were all waiting for God to pick one of us to do it but hoping our name didn't get called. The burden of it. Praying to some other deity on a side bet that it wouldn't have to be one of us. Please God send some other more responsible guy. A kindly carpenter maybe.

There's a hole in the earth

We were sitting in the sulfurous hot spring rubbing the mud they have there on our faces and going like look at me I'm a mud man I'm going to kill your entire family haha and laughing even though it wasn't that funny. Just to be somewhere else made everything lighter at first. I said the guy at the front desk had told me that there's a place not far from here where you can dive down between two tectonic plates and you dunked your head under to wash the monster off of you and came back up and said you had to piss real bad. I looked around and said it's probably fine it already smells weird.

There was some kind of earthquake that was a big thing in the 1700s the guy said and now there's a hole in the earth and the water that rushed in to fill it is all silvery and there's one part they call the Cathedral I imagine because if you get down there it probably gets you to start believing in God.

The majesty of creation and so on.

I said the continents drift a little further apart by like one inch every year according to what the guy told me and then I started thinking about how small you are and how very small all of us are and how we've been drifting apart too because it's impossible for humans to think of anything but ourselves. I thought about tectonic plates grinding against one another and it made me think about the pain in my knee which was more real to me than geology.

Are there any sharks down there you asked and I said I don't know probably. The guy didn't say anything about sharks one way or the other.

They had shark penis on the menu at the place we went the night before and everyone thought that was pretty funny so you ordered it as a gag but then you had to follow through and eat it because it was honestly very expensive and on top of that you didn't want to seem too American.

What does it taste like I asked and you said it tastes like shark penis.

It never really occurred to me until then that sharks would have penises although I guess that basically checks out. It's not like sharks just spontaneously emerge into existence. Not yet anyway.

Then I was thinking about sharks fucking for a minute.

On one of our first dates we went to see a movie at the Kendall Square cinema called *Open Water*. It's about a couple who go on a scuba diving vacation somewhere in the Bahamas I think. Somewhere near there. Near enough to there that it doesn't matter. They go to the ocean anyway. At some point ocean is just ocean.

Due to a miscount by the person leading the scuba expedition the couple emerge from the depths to realize the boat has left them behind. At first they presume that the mistake will be rectified in the way that we all do when something goes wrong. Well this is fucked but certainly order will be restored presently we think.

"Other people go on vacation and spend their days just laying around," the husband says at one point. "We have a story we're going to be telling for the rest of our lives," he goes and indeed they did it's just that their lives didn't end up being as long as they had imagined they would be.

A day is so long but a life is very short.

As they float further and further away from the original dive spot they bicker and blame one another and grasp for something different they could have done that would have saved them from this ordeal.

As if logic is a shield against chaos.

Eventually the realization that there is no order to things and that two people can in fact be left behind like this dawns on them.

I guess it's partly based on a true story about a couple in Australia this happened to although I don't think that matters for the film or for our purposes here. It's true either way.

So thirst sets in quickly and the sun burns their faces as they bob on the tide and swarms of jellyfish sting and sharks begin to circle. All that's left is for the two of them to continue living borne along on the waves for as long as they can not knowing which of them is going to die first.

To watch it happen and to describe it makes it sound horrific which it is but it's also just a sped-up version of how life works as a matter of course. There's no rescue boat coming and the sharks have spotted us. You hope you go before the person you love because you can't bear to watch it happen to them when there's nothing you can do.

It made me think just now about how a million Americans have died over the past two years from the sickness. Their loved ones sitting by helplessly watching and waiting for a different kind of drowning to begin.

It's probably not a spoiler to tell you how the film ends anymore so than it is to spoil how any life ends which is that it ends.

It's the waiting though.

Every moment thinking even now even now even now someone might be coming over the horizon to save you.

Even now.

Surely I am blessed among all others.

Later we went for a hike along some craggy mountains and a black sandy beach along the coast and I goofed around like we were in *Game of Thrones*. I'm gonna kill the White Walkers I'm gonna fuck my sister haha I said and you pretended you didn't hear me.

Someone told me they filmed it here I said. That's why I said the thing about fucking my sister.

Ok you said.

I wasn't going to fuck my sister I figured that was obvious but who knows.

When we got back to the place we were renting someone had left a baby carriage parked out front on the sidewalk with a whole baby inside of it all wrapped up warm like a burrito and I was about to shit myself but you said that was normal to do here you saw another one earlier when you went to get the coffee so thankfully the baby wasn't my problem like I imagined it was going to be. A whole hypothetical thing averted.

You looked at the baby a little longer than I thought necessary like it was a baby you knew from somewhere. An old friend from high school or something.

Also like this baby existing instead of another one was something I had engineered.

The baby looked back up at you like you were someone he knew from later on.

There was a Subway across the street and I got depressed about that for a minute then I got over it and thought about going in for lunch. I didn't go in though I thought it would represent a failure of my character of some kind.

Did you know there are no American chain restaurants in Bermuda I said. I think they think of it like an invasive species type of thing. Once you have one they multiply.

I'm going to fuck the guy at work you're worried about you said.

You didn't actually say that but I imagined you saying it in your head so then I was mad about that.

The next day we got in a van to ride out toward the mountain we were going to hike and I pretty much wanted to cry about how beautiful it all was the entire way. Not only no stores but no nothing. Lots of nothing I mean. All of nothing.

All of old. Nothing else ever.

Green and brown and white. It's too bad we didn't get to come during the aurora borealis the guy driving said and I said I've heard it's very beautiful. The sky and what have you. You should come back again some time and I said that I definitely would. I pictured the colored star mist or whatever it is in my mind and thought about how very small you are and how very small all of us are and about how the stars are like how someone can be right there but also very distant because it's impossible for humans to think of anything but ourselves.

We were going to see the site of a memorial they had set up for a dead glacier called such and such that we had watched a documentary about. They said it was the first named glacier here to melt and lose its status as a glacier. To be demoted. It wasn't the first glacier to melt but the first one that had a name which is meaningful because when things that have names die it fucks us up more than if they don't.

The hike up basically fucking sucked and I wanted to complain the whole time but I kept it to myself.

After an hour or so we finally made it.

"Memorials are not for the dead, they are for the living," one of the scientists in the movie said about the glacier. At the rate we're going all the glaciers are pretty much fucked they said. They had a little plaque there recognizing the spot of the glacier that had died and it said something like "This monument is to acknowledge that we know what is happening and what needs to be done. Only you know if we did it."

I wonder if we end up doing it or not but I guess that's not my concern.

Then the guy told me to be careful and not to get too close to the slope there because it was a steep drop and I looked over and for the first time realized how high up we were. I never wanted a parachute so badly before in my life. They should have given us all a parachute.

We should have all been born with wings. We were at one point but you know how the one guy ruined that.

It seemed like a person could fall for forever from this height.

All of a sudden nothing was beautiful anymore.

I thought about what would happen if a person fell into a pit that was deep enough that the bottom never arrived and if after a while you would adjust to the dropping and have time to reflect on how screwed you were or if instead your heart would give out after a minute or two of the falling.

If you would have phone reception and time to call everyone you loved.

Or what if we all fell into the hole as a group at the same time. Would one of us die first right there in midair next to everyone else in the descent? The living accelerating at the same horrible velocity as the dead and unable to ever leave any of them behind.

Screaming into the face of a corpse you once knew plummeting into the silvery chasm.

Pembroke, Massachusetts

We had had a fight so I stormed outside and figured I would go for a swim to cool off although it's very hard to effectively storm when you're on your way to a pool.

Carrying your little towel.

It was twilight and the water was good cold and then there was the blur of the shark right down there skirting around in the deep end and not noticing me at first.

I don't know what kind of shark it was.

You're supposed to know the specific names of things in poems. What kind of trees are native to the area to add verisimilitude.

You were in the kitchen chopping onions for a soup and crying on account of that and in the tree outside the window the tiger you had long been waiting for was drooling.

I don't know what kind of tiger it was.

I had been imagining a scenario just like this every time I got into the water since I was a child and now that it was happening it felt something like relief.

I thought you'd never arrive I said as we worked together to get me inside of its mouth.

Beacon Street

He was telling his driver about a study that had just been published in a prestigious scientific journal. Researchers had come across a potential treatment for reversing age-related memory loss by infusing spinal fluid from younger mice into older ones.

Is that right the driver said shifting in his seat.

Afterwards the older mice were better able to recall where certain things had happened to them he said. A little light would flash or an alarm would sound and the old ones would freeze up with fear just like the young ones did because they remembered again that it meant they were due to be hurt.

An air raid siren of sorts.

Before they just kind of forgot what the signals meant and stood there dumbly being electrocuted.

It could teach us something about how to better fight Alzheimer's the man in the back seat said folding and unfolding his newspaper into halves and halves again.

The plaque and tangles that build up in the brain he said.

Plaque and tangles sir the driver said.

The driver was trying to merge into the right lane but traffic was at a standstill. The street he had meant to turn on to was blocked off because of a bad accident it seemed like. There were cop cars and ambulances everywhere hungry to be filled up and a girl selling shitty one-dollar flowers was walking in the middle of the lane coming up to their car next.

They said the process of extracting the spinal fluid and transferring it from one body to the next was pretty painstaking and slow but they had hopes that they could refine it the man in the back said.

Is that right the driver said sitting up ramrod straight now looking at the approaching flower girl and raising the window thinking about buying himself some time.

Brachypteracias p.ʳoxilus

The lord is with thee

Two years into the sickness I finally caught it and I texted my boss as much and he said well that's a bummer bro but they were short-staffed and he said he needed me to come in anyway. I read the text seven times at least just savoring every word of it like when you tongue a bad tooth and I texted back and said that's gonna be a pass from me dog and then regretted saying it like that.

Thirteen minutes later when he didn't respond I texted again and I typed sorry dog backspace backspace backspace man they said I have to go to the doctor and it was a lie and I'm sure he knew it was a lie because he didn't give us health insurance but I was making $11.25–$14.50 an hour to do whatever the job was that I did.

I could be a barista for example.

Since I had the day off suddenly and wasn't feeling badly yet I rode my bike down to the beach.

In front of the long wooden bridge they built so you can walk over the protected dune where the endangered birds nest there was one of those Christians you see around all the time now that hold up signs about how everyone is going to Hell but it was an overcast day and no one was really at the beach so I wanted to be like there's probably a better place to post up right now buddy maybe the hotel on the cliff just up the road but instead I just looked him in the eye as I walked by and he looked right back at me and to my eternal shame he backed me down. OK you win that one.

There was an entire catalog of people that were supposed to be burning in the infernal pit on his sign like BLM and Antifa and Porn Addicts and Pot Smokers and Adulterers and Buddhists and Homo Huggers and Whores and Catholics and I thought wait I am pretty much every single one of those. The latter informing all of the former.

Fortunately I still know every word to say to get out of trouble with God when the time comes. I am very simply going to cry to his Mommy which is a workaround Catholics lean into regularly. Especially those of us who only ever had a mother.

Blessed art thou among women
and blessed is the fruit of thy womb Jesus Christ

I said that poem inside of my little brain as I took my sneakers and socks off and walked toward the sand to where the horse flies swarmed. Me and this guy were both saying spells at one another and they were probably canceling each other out.

The waves were waving loudly now and I remembered where I was. The sun was reflecting hard off something just off shore in an uncanny redness and I caught a whiff of this misplaced earthy smell of barn that hit me with its full olfactory transporting force despite the fact that I hadn't been to a barn in maybe ten years.

Someone had forgotten to tie down all the beach chairs and they had blown from here to there and back again. Some of them had ended up in the water and there was one bobbing perfectly upright in the shallows like you could sit on it like a throne like Poseidon's own throne but more casual than that. Poseidon on vacation.

Like the chair was looking directly at me waiting for me to make the next move. With its chair eyes.

For a while there had been a lot of trash washing up on the beach here so seeing the chairs all jacked up wasn't a big surprise. Something about the way the loop currents move I don't know. From the plastic waste island out there it would all get swirled in. Weirdly it was a lot of plastic dolls. Baby dolls. Maybe it was how the garbage disposal works when you're cleaning the sink after dinner and everything gets caught in its centrifugal force and pulled into the teeth.

I used to think the garbage disposal was a blender but I had to fuck with the one at work when it broke often enough that I finally just learned what it did. There are things called impellers or lugs down there fixed onto a spinning plate and they spin and spin and compel the organic matter inward which gets pulverized against the grinding rig very finely almost into liquid and then the running faucet flushes it all into the underground pipes and takes it to wherever all that ends up.

New Hampshire perhaps.

I knew the thing about all the dolls washing up because they had had the news come down here every now and again to do a little segment about it. You can see why the news would care about it because people would hear all that and go oh haha wow and then share it online so people would talk to them on the computer about it.

The ocean dolls would have barnacles growing out of their eyes or a bouquet of clams or mussels or scallops clustering out of their mouths like the shellfish latched on to whatever was available at hand to hide inside of.

I suppose it was fair that there was sea life inside of the plastic instead of the other way around which was how it usually worked now.

There was a whole locally popular Instagram account about it. This one lady would trawl the beach in a bikini and find all these dolls that looked like they had been left behind on the Titanic a hundred years ago and pull them out of the water and wash the sand off gently and do a video and be like hee hee what a precious little baby boy in this cutesy voice and everyone would press the button and make her numbers go up. Usually the dolls wouldn't have any of their doll hair attached anymore but the lady didn't have an answer for why that was when people would ask in the comments. So they were just bald and sort of shrunken in the face and their eyes were usually hollowed out. They looked like a guy at the bar sitting alone drinking who had seen some things.

My buddy knew the girl in college. He said she was nice. He said he almost went out with her once but maybe he was just trying to impress me and guess what it worked.

Was she like that back then I asked one time and he said no she was just some girl. Some girl writing papers. Trying to figure out how to be a person.

I went into the water and got jostled around a bit more than I was expecting. Waves typically come in from the one main direction we are all familiar with but the pattern was overlapping geometrically today like an old screensaver. The seaweed was thick like weeds in a shallow pond and the sand was quickening under my feet in a way that I didn't recognize with every inhalation of the tide. The way the sand runs over your feet like an expensive spa massage as the ocean is sucking it back inward and you dig your toes in like they're talons like it's some reflex from a million years before we were forced into these kind of bodies.

A redness was reflecting off the clouds and I got out of there with my little life and toweled off my claws with my t-shirt near where the sea lice were swarming and walked back up and across the wooden bridge and there was this fucking guy again waiting like he was proselytizing today just for me. It didn't seem efficient. I know because I'm a barista as I mentioned earlier and doing that you have to be able to multitask. Making things and breaking other things down at the same time. Always cleaning and always making a new mess at once.

I noticed Papists was another name on his list of the damned and I thought that seemed redundant with the Catholics already on there. Like I said this guy needed to streamline his entire operation.

Being prejudiced against Catholics was some real old school shit I thought as the flies from the dune edge started to find me again and tell all their friends I was back.

Weirdly I knew people who were converting to Catholicism lately at like thirty years old. I think they just wanted an excuse to be socially conservative but didn't have the courage to go all the way. Maybe the pageantry and architecture added some kind of anchoring sense of ceremony they were lacking in their lives otherwise.

The architecture was very good I wasn't going to deny that but how much can architecture actually enhance a soul at long last?

I don't think you can become a Catholic ex post facto. If you weren't born with this internal self-hatred and fear of the fire from before you could wipe your own asshole you don't get to assume the mantle and reap all the spoils such as . . .

I'll think of some of the spoils later.

I think other religions want new people to join all the time but that's a no from me dog.

Sorry I don't know why I keep saying dog.

Let me start this entire thing over.

Hell is not empty.

All the devils are not here is what I mean.

Our Catholic Hell is very very very full and the devils are busting their asses down there working overtime (non-union) torturing everyone that came before us.

As I walked back into cell signal territory I immediately had about twenty texts on my phone but I didn't check them right away since I figured it was my boss asking me to come in again because he was getting his teeth kicked in at work. Those were all the texts that ever came through.

When I looked up from my phone the guy with the sign had disappeared and there was the smell again like the mix of hay and horse shit. No wait it was pigs maybe. Little baby pigs suckling at an enormous sow's heaving milky pig tits in the mud. Milky little pig boys slurping it up and drinking until they burst. Ignorant of Heaven but happier than we'd ever known how to be.

Æschna grandis

PLATE XVIII.

Image captured October 2019

It would have been a fall day when the map car drove down our old street because the tree in the little park that you loved to post pictures of every year is there in its full striking orange on the way toward dying but not just yet.

It must have also been trash day because the bins are out front by my car which is parked in a space I wouldn't normally park in. Some piece of shit must have taken my spot. I would have been inside at the time thinking I better go pull the bins back in. Taking the bins in and out is one of the chief things a person has to do in their life.

I zoomed out and scrolled over to the main street and there's very little traffic and the light by the intersection is green and I am coasting along right now by the still-there shopfronts that burned down a few years back and never really recovered from it when they rebuilt.

The dry-cleaning place I abandoned some shirts at. The woman there had so many customers' phone numbers memorized. The sun-obliterated old posters on the walls.

It was fall too when the car took a picture of my parents' house. Further along into fall it seems because the trees there are naked and clawing the sky and there are dried leaves all over the ground and swept up onto the sidewalk with the trash thrown out of windows by people in cars passing by on their way to somewhere prettier. Cape Cod for example.

I had the brief hope I might be able to see my father out in the yard fucking around with this or that but there was no proof that he or anyone else was alive there in the image. Nothing captured for posterity.

An earlier day I drove down to see my parents in person and sure enough there was my father out in the yard fucking around with this or that. When I pulled into the driveway I beeped the little hello song on the horn and he looked at me for a minute through the windshield not knowing who I was and I got out and I said didn't you recognize me and he said that he didn't at first.

We talked for a while under a tree he was going to take down soon. There are always trees that need to be taken down for one reason or another. Maybe because they're rotted out and an eyesore or like the danger they pose of falling over and hurting someone. Taking the whole house down.

You could pay a guy to do it quicker but what they're asking to do it nowadays.

He asked me if I remembered so and so.

It's never a good sign when your parents ask you if you remember so and so because that dude is fucked.

Another time on Easter at the house I looked through a photo album my aunt had brought with her while all the children looked at their phones and every time she turned a page one of the pasted Polaroids would come off its ancient glue and she'd shuffle it back into place half-assedly and tell me about how this lady or that guy in the photos from the 1983 Halloween party had died. The clown had a skiing accident. The flapper found out a month before it was going to happen and no one believed it. My uncles there in giant eyeglasses looking like some guy I know now. Their girlfriends as stewardesses and me going hm.

This dead fella my dad knew drank himself to death he said. He was an old friend of my parents but I think they had had a bad falling out years ago and so it was less like the mourning of someone once loved than simply registering the name of the dead in a collective book we share custody of.

Keeping you up to date on who from back home is dead now is one of the main things your parents have to offer you after a certain age.

Your siblings meanwhile get to tell you who from school overdosed.

Whenever you hear that type of thing even if you don't know the guy you gotta go ah their poor kids and then the other person goes I know their poor kids.

They found him dead my dad said which is never a good sign. When you are found dead it's different than having died it implies something worse. Like no one noticed for a while that you were gone.

Then my mother woke up from her vapors and came out and cried and hugged me like I'd just returned home from war which was partly true and the last of a long line of golden retrievers my dad has loved more than he ever loved his children followed behind her and crawled into my lap and nestled her head under my chin and suggested I rub her back until she felt safe.

My dad has a shrine set up for every dog he's ever had next to his piano. There's got to be about fifteen of them from over the years. I only recognize a couple of them anymore by name.

My mother tried to make me take some massager thing she uses on her back and I said no no it's ok and she said just take it and I said I don't want to take the fucking machine Ma even though I kind of did want it. She asked me again to take my comic books that had been sitting upstairs for two decades when I left. Maybe they're worth money she said.

My parents are getting older now and sometimes I get very angry about that and it makes it difficult for me to be around them in a way. Like I'm constantly on edge. I'm not angry at them of course it's not their fault but I do selfishly find their aging to be an affront to me personally. Even though the inevitability of their passing someday hopefully at least twenty years from now is the most natural thing in the world the one single predictable thing we all have in common the fact that I have to watch it happen step by step like this until it finally arrives seems indecent. Like watching them undress.

I wouldn't have minded watching you grow old like that if I could have had the chance. Changing just so every season so slowly I barely noticed. Taking pictures of your tree.

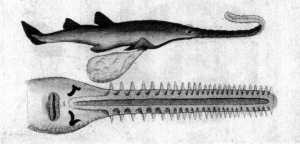

F. MDLIV. SQUALI PRISTIS.
Ein langschnäuziger Saagefisch.
L'Esturion de la Scie.
The Saw-Fish.

Hope as an anchor

The owl babies were hatching at long last right there on the live stream. In the top corner it said 350 million people were watching. People were cheering outside my window like when soccer used to still be on and I looked out and some dude was hauling ass down the street naked whooping it up to all hell. The soldiers didn't even go after him they were watching on their phones too.

You sing harmony

The water level of the lake had been receding for so long that the things people expected to stay submerged forever started to turn up on the shore. On what was newly the shore.

Some struggling boaters saw a curious rusted barrel that jutted at 45 degrees out of the shallow watery muck one day like an unexploded missile.

The authorities came down to poke their snouts around and they popped the can open and sure enough there was the body of some poor son of a bitch. What was left of it. They didn't know if it was a man or woman at first due to it had been inside of there so long. How water and time conspire against flesh. Also none of them wanted to look too closely in the way cops are lazy.

Eventually they pieced together the provenance of the fella's sneakers which had held up longer than his body. Better stitching than God's back then. We used to make things here. They estimated they were purchased from Kmart sometime in the mid-1970s and they put that fact on the TV and so now this guy was suffering one last indignity. Not as big an indignity as everything else that brought him to the barrel mind you but nonetheless.

Going forward there are going to be more bodies like this found down there the chief of police said and he was shortly proved right but if this place was such an obvious hotspot for hiding corpses what were you guys doing this whole time not fishing through it?

It didn't make a difference either way in the long run. No matter how far the lakes receded the oceans were catching up in the other direction. Water was fixing to find its level. And you and I there in the middle waiting in our expensive sneakers watching some other guy be dead first and not even recognizing we were standing in a line behind him.

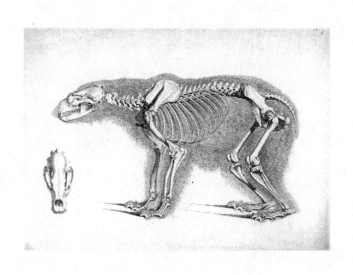

It starts a tidal wave

It was the last day it would ever snow but we didn't know it and we got into bed nice and early. Your feet so cold against me as always. We fell asleep to a silly sitcom we'd already seen five times at least. To trick our brains to be quiet.

Later it was the last time they would play the World Series but we didn't know that either and we got into bed nice and early and watched without rooting for anyone in particular.

We loved it in there. Huddling under the covers. The period before unconsciousness was a pocket out of time.

The fifteen good daily minutes we each got.

To be able to wake up the next day and reset everything and try again.

Like nothing could hurt us.

Like a child thinks.

Eventually your feet frozen so cold and me crawling back under the covers to join you after the fire went out.

I'll see you in the morning baby I whispered and I could see the words vaporizing in the cold air.

They have the largest eyes

I've never seen a dead horse in person. I read a poem recently that said when you see a living horse you're supposed to yell out horse! and if you don't it's a sign of a sociopathic mind of some kind or other.

I have oddly seen a lot of pictures of horse skeletons however which are still beautiful even half in the dirt. They still seem like they're moving like they have some other bone place to be even now.

On the TV they were impeaching the president and they said it was like the crucifixion at Golgotha. As bad as that.

Then I saw it reported that in Honolulu a cop had admitted that he had forced a man to lick a urinal if he wanted to avoid getting arrested as like a funny little cop prank. The man was an addict who had been in and out of jail for years his family told the news and he was in a documentary one time where he was checking himself into rehab saying he was going to turn things around this time and things like that the things you say and you hope are true when you say them. They weren't true for him in this case but they often aren't.

I thought for some reason for a minute that it was weird that the cops in Hawaii do the same shit they do everywhere else and that is obviously stupid because cops are the same everywhere even on beautiful islands. Maybe worse because fewer people are watching.

I don't know anything at all about Hawaii to be honest I've never seen it and I most likely never will. Here's one thing I know though: There were no horses or many land mammals of any kind on Hawaii originally they all had to be brought there by people in boats.

Years ago I told you I liked to look at pictures of horses fighting sometimes and you thought that was a weird thing to say and I said it had never occurred to me as long as I had lived for some reason that horses would fight each other but once I knew that they do it made me look at things differently. Horses mainly but also everything.

Standing back on their hind legs punching out wildly like that.

I thought we had just enlisted them all this time into our own aggression against their will. Maybe they learned it from us.

You loved me for a little while after that but not for long enough.

Another time and another version of you told me you had an imaginary horse as a pet when you were young and I loved you for that but not for long enough.

Sometimes I get it into my mind that I could fight an animal like a bear or an angry dog and I know that's stupid but I think it anyway because it's free to fantasize about anything you want. I wouldn't know where to start with a horse though.

One time not far from here someone went out and slaughtered fifteen horses with a gun.

There were dozens of them that would roam around this particular area of woods and field running around fucking each other and slooshing out horse babies and doing other horse type of business and sometimes people would go out and feed them in the winter when finding food to eat was apparently difficult for the horses.

It looked like a battlefield for horses the sheriff said and a woman who works in animal rescue went on the news and said that although she's been around and seen some terrible things in her career this was different. She said it was an act of evil for lack of a better term. As if Satan himself had stage directed it all.

She said that the horses were very friendly before they were shot to death and that you could walk right up to them and touch them when they were still alive and I suppose you could feel the horse skeleton moving underneath. You could love a horse like that for a long time but not for long enough.

And then unfall again

It was a forty-degree day in February but it had been seventy-five the day before out of nowhere so all the bugs were out in the yard tipsy and flying crooked like when the lights turn on at the club at the end of the night and people are panicking in their baseball caps and high heels about what happens next. Whether they'll have to be alone forever.

These bugs. She remembered these same guys from the year before when they first showed up. Their parents anyway. Or grandparents. Who knows how bug generations go. The gnats and mosquitoes but bigger who blew here from the deep black river full of rusted bicycles and a century of liquid capitalism a couple streets over. They were spiraling on account of the early wakeup call probably cursing in their bug words. Let me get my bug coffee first haha they said by which they meant her blood.

She thought she would kill them all if she could and then decided she would just go ahead and do it now and so started running around the yard like a crazy person with her mouth open not swatting them away but wafting them inward instead.

Her tongue unfurled two feet long and she choked them all down one by one real fast like a rodeo clown cracking a whip. She ate every single bug in the yard with a big smile on her face with her shrinking teeth receding back into her jaw and then a bunny bounded into her field of vision and froze when it smelled that she smelled it and darted away quicker than she was just yet.

Her eyes shifted on her skull back and upwards like an evil hacking plastic surgeon's work like poorly done stop-motion animation but now she could be on the alert for predators of her own in the periphery. It hurt like nothing she had ever felt and then didn't hurt anymore.

She gorged herself on the bugs tonguing the grass carpet until she was satisfied which didn't last long because it was dirty work chasing them and soon she was hungry again. A one-hundred-and-forty pound animal taking what was hers on the fifteenth day of February in two thousand and twenty five. In the window just behind her and to the side her neighbor was in his kitchen walking to the fridge with his stupid small mouth hanging open and his short useless tongue wetting. She felt like she could jump over his entire house.

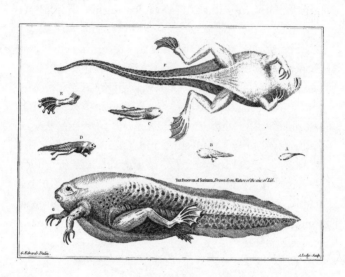

The Frog &c. of Surinam, Drawn from Nature of the size of Life.

G. Edwards Delin.

A. Loseby Sculp.

A looming conflagration

The next county over was on fire again which no one really wanted to talk about anymore. Imagine the biggest house on your block was always in flames and it burned all the time and it burned so often that you eventually just accepted as a given that there was going to be a house down the street that would be burning no matter what anyone did which was in any case not much. If firefighters were cops and when they came they just stood around and were like I don't know what to tell you champ and got pissed off about you asking them to do anything at all then kicked your asshole in.

We have to address Fire House the stern mayor would say on TV and then they would get it under control for a while until they didn't and the mayor would have to come on TV again. Goddamnit he'd say. This time I mean it.

You would get used to the smoke after a while right? It's probably not going to get me you'd think then you'd go run your errands at the store and the mayor would get in trouble for fucking someone he wasn't supposed to fuck and everyone would get preoccupied about that for a week or two.

They have incarcerated people out there fighting the fires and apparently they don't let them become real firefighters after they get out.

Not real but official I should say.

I don't know if they're afraid they're going to steal the fire or what.

Bring its gift down the mountain to the people.

I drove by one of the tent camps they were staying in during an earlier fire and I heard they sometimes work for up to 24 hours straight out there and get paid two dollars a day for their trouble while some other guys stand around with machine guns for maybe seventy-five dollars a day not doing much else.

I gather that fighting fires is a desirable job for a lot of the prisoners since you get to go outside which is a much better alternative to living inside of a cage even if the entire world is burning. At least you have a fighting chance against a fire. The hope is that you can extinguish it.

I've loved all I've needed

If you had asked people they would have said in retrospect that they had always imagined it would be a flip of a switch kind of thing like one day there would just be tornados in every direction and then they would go to lay down with the whole family in the big bed to receive their mercy. The shotgun nearby probably useless now but just in case.

Instead it was just that the wind became more impossible to ignore every day and then more again and so on.

It was kind of weird that the wind was the issue. At one point they moved the MPH thing up to the top spot on the weather app instead of the temperature and it stayed there for as long as it all worked. The satellites buzzing around us.

There had been a series of dust storms before the day in question. The type of storms that made it so you couldn't see more than a few feet in front of you. The type of storms that blocked out the sun and the streetlights and sometimes the hand in front of your face. A person could get lost out there and they often did.

After you'd find birds and varmints and even cattle in places they shouldn't be dead and strangled by the dust.

That Palm Sunday started out bright and sunny. In the midst of all that had happened it was what people would have imagined a miracle would look like.

Like the Heavens were going to open.

Like a respite from all this suffering.

Everyone had gone to the church and we did too which seemed like an admission of sorts on my part. A mea culpa if you follow me. No atheists in a world dug entirely of foxholes kind of thing. It was the beginning of the holiest week in the calendar after all. The lead up to the Resurrection.

Pretty quickly into it all there came billowing clouds of dark that relieved people of any concept of horizon. You could tell the priest was pretty enthusiastic about it all at first. Nervous like when a ballplayer gets his first at bat in the majors. Some lady wrote a couple songs about it all later but I never got to hear any of them.

We had driven over to visit our families for the last time just the day before. They stood outside and waved to us and as we left it looked like they were passing by on a slow-moving ship leaving port.

It used to be years ago that people would come in and out of your life and when they were leaving you would make plans to stay in touch but it was pretty much a gamble one way or the other how it would go. One of you maybe half lying about it.

You might mail three letters.

Then for a while with the computer you were never allowed to be rid of any single person you ever met unless they were perhaps very adamant about you doing so like the person I was hoping to meet again when this was all over somewhere else. Where we all get to start over. Where I'm sorry is a reincarnation spell.

At the bottom of it all now it was just us and the neighbors huddling together in the pews waiting for the priest or literally anyone to tell us what happens next and where we were likely leaving for. A journey isn't the trouble it's how long it's going to be and where it ends.

The front doors of the church flung open with the wind and I had this stupid idea for a second that it was You Know Who. Coming all this way to deliver us himself unto Himself. It wasn't Him though. It wasn't even the other guy. It wasn't anyone or anything at all it was just the wind.

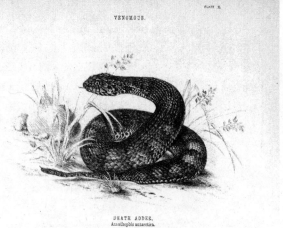

VENOMOUS.

PLATE X.

DEATH ADDER.
Acanthophis antarctica.

Helena Forde, del. et lith.

J.A. Engel, imp.

Tab.XX.

Please don't go

There had been torrential rain for hours and so the basement flooded. When she got home the man she somehow still lived with was down there with the vacuum and she said that looks kind of fun and he said I know I thought so too but it fucking sucks so she took over for a while and it was fun for about thirty seconds.

Well this fucking sucks just like you said she said.

After they filled up the bucket they took a handle on each side and carried it up through the cellar bulkhead where a thousand spiders waited and immediately dropped it spilling all of the water right back onto the floor they had just cleared. Fuck fuck she said fuck fuck and then stopped saying fuck because it wasn't worth it. She understood this would have been hilarious to watch happen to someone else but not so much to her specifically. To them both she meant. Tragedy needs a while in the oven to complete its famous metamorphosis.

She went back to work with the vacuum again anyway thinking the last thing I need right now is for my basement to become a metaphor for anything.

The water was seeping up through the stone now with no obvious source like the house was bleeding. It looked like a Koji Suzuki story down there.

Under one pole that held the too-low ceiling up there was an especially bad gusher and she pointed the vacuum at it like a surgical assistant and it sucked and

160

sucked and she just could not drain the thing it was like a weeping wound it was like trying to vacuum the ocean but she was determined to beat it she became sort of maniacal about it like a person bailing a sinking boat out because no one else was going to do anything and the alternative was swimming down there forever.

Thy kingdom come

It was agreed upon that there would be no more drinking for the time being so we gathered up the bottles from each apartment and locked them in a closet in the basement. One last kick in my asshole from democracy.

The fighting hadn't reached the city yet but it was on the way. Like tracking a package delivery on your phone. En route. Ten minutes away. We've left it outside your door.

One wanted to forestall despair and to stay sharp was why and besides there were all these guns around all of a sudden and none of us with much in the way of training. No point accidentally blowing your own head off at a time like this when some pig dick was on his way to do it for you in short order.

I took one last heroic swig as I locked up the door and felt the warmth run through me then regretted it then didn't regret it or anything anymore for a little while.

After a period of quiet and fucking with our phones to try to get a signal we got to talking about the things we'd always hoped we'd have had a chance to do. Cities around the world we'd wanted to visit. Things like that.

I never got to see New York R. said. I know it's not like it is in the movies but still you know. The energy.

R. was so beautiful I wanted to kill myself about it.

W. was our landlord and had been a bigshot at the university and since I never finished my studies there I had a hair across my ass about his whole thing.

I thought I could've cut his throat and no one would say anything about it but I had no justifiable reason to do that. I wouldn't do something like that actually.

F. was looking at me like I was an asshole and he loved me but he could've broken me in half if he wanted to and he often wanted to so I untensed my shoulders.

I don't know why I thought something like that about W. It was the booze in the closet that had gotten to me. I never stopped knowing it was just there the entire time we waited. A vampire sensing a heartbeat. The agony of that.

L. was trying to breastfeed in the corner but having an awful time of it from what I could tell.

Why don't you say a poem for us someone asked W. and he coughed and cleared his throat and said ah well at a time like this etcetera.

I know one I said.

> *Margaret, are you grieving*
> *Over Goldengrove unleaving?*
> . . .
> *It is the blight man was born for.*
> *It is Margaret you mourn for.*

That wasn't the type of thing I would normally do. That was weird of me to do.

Manley Hopkins! W. said seemingly impressed. Clapping like a hog.

I'm not stupid I wanted to say. I'm not so fucking stupid and in my head I was throttling him and hanging him over the balcony but not really meaning it. I think you understand me.

I don't remember many poems anymore but that one was always easy to remember because it rhymed so simply and obviously which I guess was the point of inventing rhyming in the first place. So that we wouldn't forget things. To pass down and like that.

W.'s wife was always kind to me before she passed. I got the sense she was watching this all transpiring from somewhere and decided I better act more normal. Curses aren't real but what is the point of chancing it. God isn't real either but same idea.

I looked at R. to see if she had any type of look on her face about the poem I said or not.

Idiot. A woman doesn't want to marry a poet. Not if they have any sense about anything. Maybe sleep with one for a while before smartening up. Poems are for the very young and for the very old not for people in the very middle like me which is maybe why I don't remember too many of them anymore. Maybe they'll all rush back to me toward the end if there's time.

Before the shooting started dozens of us were dying every day from the sickness. Prisoners were set free to shovel the bodies into pyres and the smoke got so thick and corrosive sometimes that it felt like the sun had set at 3 in the afternoon. Everyone knew we were breathing in the dust of our neighbors but no one ever said it out loud. It seemed like a further offense to them to acknowledge what was happening.

We'd long since stopped watching the TV for news. The main channel had signed off the other day and left a music video playing over and over and not even an overtly political one as far as I could tell so I'm not sure what the point of that was.

Everyone always wants something to mean something.

After some time had passed it was decided one of us should go upstairs and peek out the window to see what all we could see and I said I would do it almost too enthusiastically but everyone seemed relieved about it so I climbed to the fourth floor and let myself into my apartment and found a small flask I had stashed away and drank from it and felt pretty much fine about the whole thing just then.

How nothing can hurt you.

An explosion went off somewhere far enough away that it didn't matter. We got pretty good about judging that sort of thing. The speed at which sound can travel.

I have a recurring nightmare where I'm dangling off the side of a building or a cliff or something like an action hero and I'm barely holding on to someone I love below me trying to pull them back up to safety but I'm not strong enough and they fall to their death I presume but it all blacks out before they land.

You can't be going around thinking about that type of shit all the time when you're awake though.

I have another dream where there's a horse underneath my bed. It doesn't do anything it just lays there like a sick horse breathing badly. Its massive rib cage moving in and out. It's almost peaceful like the sound of the ocean but if I'm honest I've seen the ocean only the once so what do I know.

I slid the glass door to the balcony open and poked my head out and it was snowing and then it was raining and then it was sunny and then it was snowing again. Down below someone was running along the street pushing a baby stroller. Not fleeing or in a panic or anything just jogging. She had a bright red hat on and I waved down to her but she must not have seen me because she just kept going.

A recycling bin was blowing around on its wheels in the wind like a malfunctioning robot and I practiced pointing my gun at it and imagined how it would fall over if I shot. I wanted to shoot it so badly but I decided I better save the bullet.

I made the sign of the cross and closed my eyes then snapped out of it and noticed the pile of dirty dishes in the sink I assume would just stay there forever now.

Maybe not. Maybe we would be saved at some point. One had to think that.

You had to think that.

I hadn't been to church in a long time before I prodigally returned when things started to get peculiar last year and it turns out they had changed the wording of the Lord's Prayer ever so slightly in the intervening years since I was a regular and whenever I heard it spoken differently it was alien to me it was like if you went to karaoke and found out they had changed the lyrics to "Don't Stop Believing" behind your back and told everyone else but you.

When I went back downstairs everyone was quiet so I said why don't we say a prayer and we all held hands and felt strange about it but said the words anyway.

Thy kingdom come.
Thy will be done.
On Earth as it is in Heaven . . .

The general consensus before all of this started seemed to be that we were waiting for some ideal version of ourselves to finally arrive and right the wrongs of the previous generations but that always struck me as a form of postponing the inevitable. A type of punting.

I think that we are now in this cruel and unforgiving and merciless moment of unchecked violence and sickness and indifference to others the people we were always going to be and always have been no matter how many billions of prayers or poems we've said. I think the ideal version of this country is here now. It's a train we've been waiting to board that we've already been traveling on for miles we just didn't realize it yet.

Saying the prayer seemed to give everyone something to reflect on for a while so I sat there quietly thinking about who I would have to kill around here to get one more drink.

Neither deer nor the woods

Someone down at the computer company had entered the numbers in wrong is what he said. I didn't fully understand it but my son tried explaining it to me anyway. He said long story short the code had been put in upside down and so now the phones were acting weird and showing me pictures in my feed of memories that hadn't yet come to pass.

Innocuous things at first mostly.

A gorgeous grilled sandwich with thick strips of bacon and plump salted sweating tomatoes with the gooey cheese melting over the toasted rye at a pub in Portsmouth I guess we're going to be going to next year.

The birth announcements of couples I didn't even know were together never mind expecting and a monstrous storm off the nearby rock-spiked coast and the aftermath with the waves tall enough for some daredevils to surf while I apparently looked on from the safety of the shore.

A rainbow wider than the world below it.

My dear old aunt passing. She loved me more than she ever was required to and I never forgot that.

Each image was something like a lucid dream you've just woken up from and are glad to be outside of but desperately want to return to. A stove that burned you yes but not so badly you wouldn't consider touching it again just to be sure.

Also they were still serving me targeted advertisements in between each post and that didn't seem ethical in my opinion.

Then there was a photo I must have taken at a museum somewhere of Bosch's *The Temptation of Saint Anthony*. I wasn't the type of person who would go to a museum in . . . I don't even know where that's from. My son had to tell me who the artist was and then I had to look up what was going on inside of the painting and in one section there are two people riding a fish in the sky and down below is a naked woman hanging out with a toad and she's beckoning toward the saint and he's sort of looking out at all of us the viewers like are you seeing this come on what am I supposed to do here with this broad? When you're at a bachelor party and your buddy is acting foolish and you go I don't know man don't look at me for help. You wanted this.

In the background are some windmills.

My grandmother used to make us say a prayer to this guy every time we couldn't find something we had lost and it worked just frequently enough that she could be like see I told you.

Scrolling along there was a photo of me and you at a Celtics game looking so happy and I tried zooming in to scan the rafters to see if another banner had been hung by the time it was taken but the angle was all wrong.

Your hair looked so nice put up like that you would have spent some time on that.

Now a fishing trip on some cold black water that me and the boy went on together and I felt him feeling pity for me in the photos like he knew something about me and next was a deer approaching from the edge of a wood that meant nothing to me in terms of memory. Neither deer nor the woods. Not memory but the opposite of that. You know what I mean. A premonition is a memory of sorts. In the general memory bloodline anyway.

Both those images were a touch blurry. I never got any better at photography it looked like. I had meant to do that. I was going to retire and do that.

And there's me gaunt in a hospital bed and under the photo I wrote for some reason:

Don't be scared haha. This is what I look like now.

I wrote that to my two hundred and twelve friends and there's a bright orange cat sitting in my lap which doesn't seem right because I was never a cat person and besides that can't be ok with the hospital rules-wise you'd think. I have no idea how old I am in that photo I could be sixty or one hundred thousand years old.

There's a scant reflection of someone taking the picture in the glass of the framed watercolor hanging above the bed behind me and I am trying to make out if it's you just now because you show up in fewer and fewer of the photos as the timeline inches forward.

God please it has to be you. Jesus please I mean. No one else should be taking that picture. I should not appear in any pictures you weren't there to see.

Now a photo of a cup of pudding on a sterile tray. Another with an oxygen tube in my nose and me giving the finger to show I'm still myself. Still the type of guy who would do that.

The boy called me later that night and said they had fixed the bug in the code and if I rebooted my machine it would all go back to how it was before and I was going to do it but not just yet I still had the rest of my life to recoil from for a little while.

Jesus Christ is that how things go? Not just for me but for everyone.

I'm not swearing when I say it like that I'm praying.

LE CHAT DES BOIS PLUS, ... Animal de Callliopee ou chien d'Orne

Jane Doe 2

There was some kind of rare rainbow that was supposed to be a big deal outside that everyone was posting pictures of. She didn't pay attention at first because she was busy cultivating her maladies. After a while when no one would shut the fuck up about it she steadied herself reaching out to the walls of the hallway to tremble out to the porch and there it was just where everyone said it would be. It looked like they were playing Mario Kart in Heaven and she fell down to her knees which to be fair she often did as a matter of course but this time with meaning behind it and no word of a lie she wept looking up at the big dumb sky. She didn't know what the sky was even made of. Every day we look up at it and no one knows what it is. No one knows what anything is and we still have to do all of this for as long as we possibly can just choosing every day to defy the alternative.

A plane from Logan flew across the expanse of the full sky rainbow like a bug crawling along the TV at night with its internal compass screwed. Trying to navigate by the light of an artificial moon. She reached out to swat it away and felt it crunch in her swift hand.

A stick figure throwaway gag

I was at the Oscars and I ducked out to a bar nearby that I assume that they still have somewhere around there. A dive bar but it's clean and they have good beer and everyone there is nice to you but not too nice.

I wanted to check on the Celtics score and I noticed Kirsten Dunst was there too taking a breather from the ceremony and then next thing she and I were talking about Marcus Smart as Defensive Player of the Year.

She was born in New Jersey then grew up in Los Angeles but she thought that the Celtics were really cool she told me. She always thought guys from Boston were handsome.

I asked her if she remembered when she was in that one movie *Melancholia* and she laughed.

I figured I was killing it already and that this was basically my shot. I had just watched it last night.

What is Lars von Trier like I asked and she said he was a big Celtics fan too then Jaylen Brown darted to the hoop and scored and got the foul and the whole bar was going crazy. Right there in Los Angeles.

Watching that movie felt like plummeting in an airplane for three hours straight I said. I never want to do it again but I will never stop thinking about it.

I slept terribly the night before because I kept worrying about the film and I thought two things which were I need to write something immediately and I don't think it's probably worth writing anything ever again.

My good friends had had a baby earlier that day at the hospital down the street I told her. This was the first time I would lie to Kirsten Dunst.

I have two children with my husband Jesse Plemmons from *Friday Night Lights* and *Breaking Bad* she said.

Yeah I know who he is I said saying it kind of shitty.

I went to high school with Taylor Kitsch who played Tim Riggins I told her and she said oh that's wild where was that and I said in Canada probably.

I thought you were from Boston?

I'm not sure if anyone else picked up on this but the movie *Melancholia* was supposed to be about depression. I'm pretty perceptive about cinema. I also thought it was nice to see what the end of the world might look like in a film where Iron Man doesn't exist for a change. Would have been better for Kirsten Dunst and them if he had but you know what I mean.

Maybe even Iron Man would've been fucked with that whole thing I suppose.

The thing is the end of the world is in fact coming slowly and that is what is scary to me whether it's the actual end of all earthly existence like in the film or just the end of your own life which is basically the same thing from a personal perspective.

When David Berman died I looked up everything he ever did like you do when someone dies and I saw a comic he drew once that was titled "At the End of the World" and in one of the panels there's a happy looking stick figure sitting straight up in a stick figure hospital bed with a stick figure sun shining through the stick figure window and beneath it all it says:

The terminally ill perk up.

The terminally ill perk up is an ocean man. It's an entire novel in a stick figure throwaway gag. The world was already ending for them soon but now it was ending for everyone and in that they've been made just like the rest of us. It might seem sinister in a way but it's not it's a sort of comfort in knowing that you don't have to die alone anymore you get to die with everyone else at the same time.

It's finding out you belong again.

You weren't singled out to suffer after all.

I guess that is what happens to Dunst's character in the second half of the movie. She is terribly depressed throughout so depressed she doesn't even want to fuck Alexander Skarsgård anymore but the arriving apocalypse provides a salve of sorts and it proves her right too in a way in thinking that nothing mattered all along.

A gazelle in a nature documentary jumping up so high and so quickly sideways while the lioness lunges. So many beautiful useless jumps.

I looked up how to spell Alexander Skarsgård just now to double check and it showed a picture of him with his shirt off and now I don't want to finish writing this story anymore or do anything. I shouldn't have ordered me and Kirsten Dunst that basket of onion rings.

I just remembered that a couple years ago at a Tennessee Titans game they honored David Berman on the scoreboard due to he was a big fan of the team and it made me cry a little when I saw that. They wrote up on the board "Nashville (and the world) will always love David Berman! 1967–2019."

A guy like that being honored at a football stadium.

The Celtics were up 20 in the fourth but Kirsten Dunst was starting to lose interest in me.

I told her the movie was excruciating and I somehow wanted it to end and never wanted it to end kind of like how I feel about all of this.

I told her about how I picked up my best friend from the hospital one time real late at night and he said sitting there in the pathetic little socks they give you he said you know the funny thing is I don't even want to die and I said I believe you. I told him I believed him Kirsten Dunst.

Playing dead

A childhood friend had died and we were sharing photos in the group chat going remember this and remember this like you do when someone dies and here was one of us at Boy Scout camp a certain number of years ago. There we all were in our tight green cargo shorts and the socks pulled up high with everything else that would ever happen to us still to come and I thought of climbing trees and digging holes and rowing boats and shooting arrows and running three-legged races etcetera but the one memory that has stuck with me the most from my half dozen summers out there in the stolen state forest was from my first night ever away at camp. I would have been about twelve or thirteen and I was getting set up in my tent and I was nervous to be away from home and I had to go to the bathroom real bad and so I walked a safe distance out into the thicket where no one could see me and squatted next to a tree and emptied fifteen pounds of turds directly back into my dropped shorts. A marksman couldn't have hit a more direct bullseye. Not a single drop made it onto the ground.

It was like pitching a perfect game.

After I had buried the evidence in a shallow grave and cleaned myself up for what felt like four hours I told my dead friend what had happened and he said you idiot there's a bathroom we're supposed to use just down the path over there.

So my training as an outdoorsman was off to an inauspicious start.

A couple days later I shot a gun for the first time and did some Native American themed ceremony stuff that probably wasn't great in retrospect and then one night my dead friend and I slept directly under the bright celestial canopy with the entire universe as our blanket. I never felt more anchored to the earth. That I'd have to suffer under the boot of its cursed gravity for as long as I lived and never once breathe in how a second planet's air tasted.

There was a noise in the near distance that sounded like an animal and this other child asked me if I thought there were bears out there and I said yes of course to sort of scare him. Putting the flashlight under my chin.

Turn that off he yelled at me and he meant it sincerely so I did. Like the effect of the light was echoing back at him from later on.

There were certain types of bears you were supposed to confront. For one you would make yourself seem big and loud to back them down and certain types you were supposed to play dead for and neither of us could remember which kind was which lying there in lower-class outer space. How the hell was I supposed to know the difference between species of bears? I didn't even know how to shit in the woods correctly which is something people and bears have been doing for millions of years without incident.

I'm just gonna run for it either way my dead friend said. I know you're not supposed to but I'm going to take off running if I see one he said which I considered a personal offense because he was always so much faster at everything than me.

The bulk movement of air

We dragged the tree inside from the cold like it owed us money and set a bowl of water out for it so it could drink and pretend it was still alive for a little while longer pretend it had a future and then a few days passed and we still couldn't find the goddamned box of lights in the wet basement so it stood there in the corner in its nakedness.

Looking up from your phone you said an acre of Christmas trees provides enough oxygen for eighteen people and they say that young trees grow very rapidly and have a higher rate of photosynthesis than older trees which is the opposite of what I would have thought. I thought being old was where it was at in the tree game.

You read to me that for a short while if it's well fed with light and water the tree will continue to produce oxygen even after it's cut down but before long the needles will dry and begin to fall off.

Later in the spring when I'm gone you might find some of them lingering in a strange corner of the house or under the flap of the rug and you will think how did this get in here and if you've remembered to buy a broom by then you'll sweep them back out into the out there out where the wind is going to be.

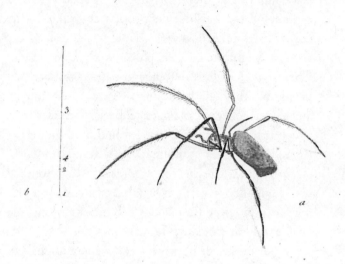

Epeïra Clavipes.

You can't take it with you

I awoke early enough for the first time in recent memory to see the last of the sunrise spilling out over the roof of the house next door in its twee little pink mist and I thought to myself sure enough there is the sunrise. I don't know if I was expecting a more profound thought than that but that was the size of it and before long it was gray and overcast again anyway and the old man next door was scurrying around fiddling with his truck getting it started and scraping the ice off of the windows.

Good morning he said.

Good morning I said.

He's got a really thick French-Canadian accent but I don't think that matters here. He's also got an old man's crush on my wife but he told us a couple times that his own personal wife had died many years ago and here he was still living despite that fact and so I thought it was basically acceptable. Let him have at least that.

I went to set my iced coffee down on the little table next to my chair on the porch and I chunked the entire thing over and I watched it happen from a remove in slow motion and I said fuck and then I had to deal with that. Everywhere else around the porch was covered in wet ice but you can't have wet ice in this particular spot that is just how it works. Things belong in their place.

Earlier maybe an hour or so before that I remember being in bed and reaching over to make sure she was still there in the way I do and she was and then I remember reaching over again and she wasn't there this time she was clattering around in the bathroom getting ready for work and I thought about how much effort it would take to go back to sleep again with my little videos of the ocean and the rain playing on the computer so I said fuck it and I figured I'd get up and have a nice coffee without expecting anything bad to happen to it.

A friend called that I haven't spoken to since the early days of the pandemic back when you would call your friends or Facetime them and such and they'd go like what the fuck is going on ha ha ha and you'd go I don't know ha ha ha back before millions of people died.

He's sober and I told him that I had been trying not to drink lately with only a little bit of success.

I told him my problem is that when I do not drink I am constantly aware of the fact that I am going to die every second of the day and that someday best case scenario like thirty years from now although probably twenty at best at this rate for me I am going to get sick in a way that there's no coming back from and she will be there when I get the phone call from some doctor I just met and I'll cry and cry with self-pity over all the bad decisions I made that brought me to this point and she'll try to console me but it won't work because hugging doesn't curtail oblivion.

I think the idea of all of this living is to accumulate enough loving and having been loved experience points that you can cash them in in one fell swoop at the end for an ameliorating effect on the descent but the prospect of that never brings me any comfort because it's all erased on the other side of it anyway. A new ledger in which your balance isn't zero it's nothing. I guess there isn't even a ledger anymore actually.

People say you can't take your money with you when you die but you can't take your love with you either.

They could wheel your deathbed out to the middle of a football stadium with the tubes and machines and nurses and everything on the 50-yard line and the stands could be full with everyone cheering and crying and you would still be down there thinking well I suppose it could be worse but what good is all this going to do me a couple hours from now?

If all this death of late has made nothing else clear to me it is the reality that you can get sick in such and such a way that there is nothing to be done about it even if you are under the care of a doctor that really or more likely mostly doesn't want you to die. They are very busy these doctors.

I know that seems like an obvious thing to realize and I am sure I always already knew it but it's not the type of thing you want to walk around being aware of all the time so when you do think of it again it hits afresh like a tossed punch.

If you want an idea of the future and also the past and the present picture a fist punching in a face but drain any sort of larger meaning from it. A fist without metaphor. Every day it's just guys getting punched in the face. Queuing up like in a depression-era bread line at the face-punching factory.

You think most days that when something bad happens they're going to marshal the heavens and earth for your benefit like you're the governor or something but that's awfully naive. It seems more likely at most they'll give it a pretty good go. Like when your car won't start you still try to turn it over a few times to be sure then maybe you check the oil and one other thing you know how to do and then are like well fuck I'm out of ideas here.

When I do drink I told my friend on the phone there if you remember him from before I said I still know that I'm going to die and that we're all going to die but it just doesn't seem like my problem for a little while and what comfort there is in that.

It's probably somewhat better to be in a plane crash whacked out on sleeping pills than wide awake for it is what I mean. Despite the fact that the destination is ultimately the same. Everyone heading into the ground I said.

He laughed in a knowing way with that superpower of self-knowledge that people in recovery sometimes have and he probably said something wise or helpful but I forget what it was because I was too busy thinking about myself.

He said he had a new job and it was going pretty well and I said that's good.

I may be repeating myself here with this I'm scared to die shit but what other story is there? Not just now at this point in time for me and you during the pandemic but for anyone at any time ever I mean.

We fat all creatures else to fat us, and we fat ourselves for maggots.

There are supposed to be anywhere between three and seven types of basic conflicts in literature. The most common are man versus man and man versus nature and man versus self. Then you might throw in man versus society or man versus the supernatural and a few other variations if you want to be fancy about it.

The third one there is the thing.

Maybe I'm just thinking about it through that lens because I just watched an episode of *Station Eleven* last night that made it obvious that that fictional post-pandemic story has been an obvious allusion to *Hamlet* the whole time. I mostly came to understand that by all the explicit references in the show to the text of the famous play *Hamlet*.

Before that I read an essay about getting sober during the pandemic and one thing the woman wrote was this: "The truth is that most of my drinking and using had one primary purpose: to allow me to feel less. To be less aware."

I thought ah come on that's my bit but I suppose there aren't too many variations on the theme when it comes to this shit.

Sometimes I'll talk to other friends in recovery and I'll be preemptively embarrassed by how cliché my whole thing probably sounds as if I'm describing the plot to a movie everyone in the world is already aware of. Like trying to surprise someone by telling them Darth Vader turns out to be Luke's father and then they have to act gracious about receiving that information from you. Oh wow. And he jumped into what now? With his hand cut off? That's fucked up!

Almost immediately after I spilled the coffee it had turned to near frozen slush in the cold air and I wondered again why we torture ourselves living through this four or five months a year. I keep having this daydream about moving to Florida our worst and most American state and while I am not under the illusion that everything that is bad still wouldn't be bad and in many ways worse there at least my hands and feet would be filled with hot circulating blood all of the time.

The last time we went to Florida we drove up the Keys to Miami in a stupid rented convertible and I gawked at the ocean for hours like who could ever get enough of this but that's stupid to think. I realize that after a while even the ocean disappears into the background when you live next to it for long enough.

I remember climbing up a narrow winding staircase inside of some lighthouse and becoming struck with a fear of the height to the point of paralysis. Not that the structure itself was going to collapse but that in order to stop the pressure compounding in my brain I would jump. If only to get the entire thing over with.

Do you ever lay there thinking about things you don't want to think about and the harder you try not to the more inevitable it becomes?

"Try to pose for yourself this task: not to think of a polar bear, and you will see that the cursed thing will come to mind every minute," Dostoevsky wrote.

That observation was extrapolated on by a psychologist in the 1980s in a famous experiment you've likely heard of where he asked subjects to not think of a white bear and to ring a bell every time that they did. You can probably guess what happened next.

The concept came to be known as ironic process theory as he explained it. I always thought when I said my brain was irony poisoned it meant something else.

In short the ironic tension here is the harder our brain tries not to think of something the more often it checks in to make sure we aren't thinking of it thereby making us think of it.

Sometimes I'll think to myself hoo boy doing a great job not drinking tonight and then a second later it's like ahh fuck I shouldn't have been aware of what was transpiring here.

No such problem when you're drinking.

Edgar Allan Poe was born in 1809 in Boston and then he died forty years later in Baltimore drunk in the gutter as the story goes. Before that his father abandoned him and his mother died young from tuberculosis and so he was taken in by John and Frances Allan of Virginia the latter of whom died and then he married his uhh thirteen-year-old cousin who also died of tuberculosis.

Newspapers attributed Poe's death to "congestion of the brain" or "cerebral inflammation" which I gather are euphemisms for alcoholism but also kind of funny sounding combinations of words you have to admit.

Congestion of the brain.

The point is this morning I came across a story of his called "The Imp of the Perverse" that I had forgotten about.

It starts out with this sort of rambling nineteenth-century pseudo-scientific jargon section about phrenology and God and what have you but then transitions into the confession of a murderer.

The thing is there was never any need for him to confess. He clearly could have gotten away with the murder in question but he was compelled against his own self-interest to do so.

The cause of the narrator's undoing Poe writes is that he is among the many "uncounted victims of the Imp of the Perverse."

The themes of confession to a crime and motiveless crime itself would carry on throughout Poe's work as well as Dostoevsky's rather famously. The general idea of this piece also comes into play in Freud's concept of the death drive.

It's weird by the way that you could just be some guy writing a story about some other guy you made up back then and accidentally invent a field of psychological study.

Poe's character explains more. He says it's like the compulsion you feel standing overlooking a great drop.

"And because our reason violently deters us from the brink, therefore do we the most impetuously approach it."

There's an important distinction in here. It's not the Imp that inspires Poe's narrator to commit the murder in the first place. That impulse is driven by his own normal human greed and cruelty. It's the Imp rather that convinces him to destroy himself afterwards because he knows that he rightfully has it coming sooner or later.

We do these actions, he writes, "because we feel that we should not."

Snakes

The Mall of Louisiana was trending and she thought oh here we go again and then she clicked on it and it turned out it was because a python was on the loose and she let out a sigh of relief because it was only a twelve-foot-long monster and not some guy. At least a monster will only attack when it's hungry.

XLVII

You were in handcuffs of your own outside of my cell
crying but trying not to and listening to me behind the
hunk of sturdy steel door set into the very old stone
walls underground having my ass ripped to all hell by
their very worst guys. After three days although you
wouldn't have been allowed to know this I honestly
learned something strange about myself for the first
time which is that I wasn't going to say shit. I had
answered the question every person wonders about
themself and there was nothing more to know. I was
more surprised about this than anyone never having
been any sort of hardened character. If I had broken
after the first day I know you would have understood.
I was near death now in any case whether it was going
to be a noble one or not it didn't change that it was
arriving sooner than later. Perhaps they had some more
inventive means of flaying they were saving for the
encore but beyond that prospect this was going to be
how it was and ever would be. I believed for a while that
my torturer respected me for my stubbornness which
may have been a myth I wove for myself to temper the
descent. I will give you a choice the primary jailor said
some days later and the choice was he said I could live on
here in this chamber with business going on per usual
with the torturing and mangling and carrying on for as
many more days as I could withstand it or else I could
be set loose into the scorched desert above ground with

you by my side where we would meet a certain death within hours either by our own rapidly deranging hand or else a more desperate clawed one waiting there in the cactus brush. Or perhaps not. Perhaps to live.

Perhaps to live.

The way in which he offered me this choice confused me because he seemed to think there was ever going to be any other decision but the one I was always going to make. In that moment I even felt pity for him. To not even have known the gift of futile hope like this which is what life was from our first breath.

PTEROPUS ROSTRATUS.

The contraption

We yanked a caveman out of the door in the contraption and got very jazzed about that for a second but then he keeled over and died before I could even poke him for a good vein so I had to fuck with the settings for a while and we tried it again.

The next one we had to all team up to keelhaul him out like a tug of war situation. This cave gentleman was stronger than a moose I swear to Christ. I basically threw out my shoulder doing it. So he came out and looked around for a few minutes breathing so calmly it was unnerving like he knew in his soul he had been here before.

To get out in front of this issue right up top we weren't clear as of yet in terms of legal on the matter of whether cavemen had souls.

Then he looked me directly in the eye and made a sound like when you shut the dog's tail in the car door by accident and died too so morale was cratering at this point so late in the game as you might imagine.

Dave said why don't you go in there and see what all is happening and I said no way I'm going in there Dave. Fucking Dave by the way. But once it was clear no one else was going to volunteer I did it. To set a good example and so forth.

Next we lassoed a medieval peasant out and he seemed hale and hearty and managed to take a few steps around and the other Dave got an idea and went over to his workbench and grabbed the can of diet soda he had been saving for lunch and offered it to the guy. Dave 2 opened the can and took a sip to show him it was ok so this dirty scared thirsty guy stood there looking at us and tried the cola and you guessed it he died instantly.

But kind of happy in dying I thought for a moment. I put down in my notes that he seemed happy for a moment.

Still I was pretty pissed off at the other Dave about that off-book move. I was trying to remember if people had been saved yet by this guy's time. If he had been baptized or not or if it was straight to purgatory with the rest of the infants and infidels.

Maybe try not setting it so far back original Dave said so I adjusted the dials and we stood back and lowered our visors and tried again and waited and after a few minutes who comes out but a full-on Nazi with the whole uniform and everything. All the medals. The little gun on his hip. We were all standing there doing side-eye like can you believe this fucking guy.

All things considered this Nazi seemed to be holding up fairly well compared to the other lot and he started yelling at us in German which we didn't understand. I said go get Martha who had studied in Stuttgart.

The Nazi was making us antsy I won't lie about that and then he was talking with Martha and shouting real staccato at her and pointing around with his other hand on his holster and she was looking over at us harried-like and doing the hand under the throat gesture like get this guy offstage but trying to be sneaky about it so I went over and got the ax. It was still dirty from ten iterations of this and I'd have to talk to the team about that.

I didn't want to do it on account of the miracle of science we had just perpetrated with respect to towing this Nazi into the future present but there were ethics to consider and after all who he was as a person so then long story short it was like now what.

To be honest I was starting to think we weren't going to be able to find an ideal type of guy to withstand this kind of torture.

Maybe instead of pulling people forward we should try the other way around it occurred to me. I looked over at Dave and I saw him seeing me gripping the ax a little tighter.

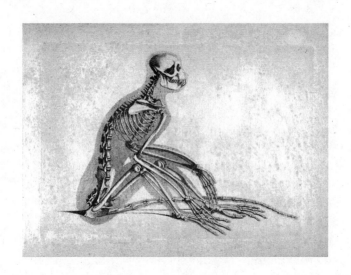

Saint Elizabeth's Hospital

Every so often I'll go in to see a new orthopedist or spine doctor and this thirty-two-year-old guy in his comfortable sneakers will go oh yeah I have a bad back too I know how you're feeling bro and it's like wait did I come to the wrong place? You literally work at the back store.

I don't know maybe they want you to register their capacity for empathy or something but it always feels like eating at an emaciated chef's restaurant.

This doctor today told me about his back but I wasn't seeing him for that kind of pain it was on the other side. Front pain. No one calls it front pain. No one says I've got a bad front. I happen to have a bad front but no one says that.

He said what he was going to do was called a quadratus lumborum nerve block and he kept telling me he wanted me to Google it and I said I would later on so he'd shut up. Essentially it's shooting steroids into your muscles so the nerve stops sending pain signals to your brain.

It's so stupid they haven't figured out how to turn all of that off by now. What are we doing here? All the smart guys inventing different kinds of websites to steal people's money on instead. Different kinds of phone cameras.

Here now were the same two nurses I usually see when I come in fucking around with this or that as

I was taking off my shirt and climbing up onto the table. One of them is named Rosemary I am fairly certain. She's a sturdy old Irish broad like a caricature of a nurse from a beloved but now problematic UK sitcom but she's nice to me and I forget the other one's name but she basically monitors my heartbeat is what her job is. While it's all happening. So everyone knows I'm still alive.

How you doing there she always asks me and I always lie and go ah it's not so bad dear because one doesn't want to seem cowardly or weak even in situations like this. These people have seen five thousand patients with blood gushing out of their necks like a geyser like in an edgy adult comic book or else an army of sturdy men crying for their mothers but I was going to impress them with my Massachusetts Catholic stoicism. They'd be decompressing later in the hospital break room having their Dunkin Donuts for lunch and they'd go that one guy now that was a proper lad. Plus he was fit. If I were twenty years younger etc they would go. They'd tell one of the younger nurses about me and she'd look like a nurse in a porno.

Here too were the pair of doctors working on me one of which was in training and so still a dumb fuck as far as the nurses were concerned based on the movement of their eyes and then the main doctor who is in charge of fighting all of the pain for everyone who comes onto this particular floor of this particular city hospital. The opposite of Batman. You'd think the Joker is the opposite of Batman but they both hurt people just for different reasons. He was facing an uphill battle anyway based on my experience of walking around this neighborhood every day smoking cigarettes outside of the coffee shop and smoking cigarettes outside of the YMCA. The people who weren't in so much pain all the time didn't come here they went to a nicer hospital I didn't have access to for their boutique agonies.

They had an ultrasound thing going and it showed them the insides of my guts up there on the computer running Windows so they would know how many layers of muscle they had to puncture the very long needle through and the main doctor kept saying to me see that see right there that's the bird's beak is what he kept calling it. That's the bird's beak he said. I guess it's a space where three abdominal muscles meet and they look like a bird's beak according to this doctor. Do you see the bird's beak he kept asking me and I was laying there on my side in the cold and getting colder room with my pants halfway down around my asshole and my shirt off gushing sweat out of my armpits because there was a huge needle inside of me squirting medicine onto my fucked-up nerves and I looked up at the screen and sure enough there it was. The bird's beak just where he said it was right there inside of me and on the computer at the same time. It was like when your friend wants to show you a funny video and he goes wait for it. No hold on wait. It's coming. Then it's like some kid breaking his neck on a water slide. I didn't need to see that you think.

Oh yeah I see it I said. The bird's beak I said.

The bird's beak he said.

The weird thing about this pain doctor is that he kept asking me during and right after the puncturing of my guts if I was feeling any better and I was like man you literally just did the thing one second ago it takes a little time right? He was a musician stopping a song halfway through for the early applause. The crowd clapping politely but awkwardly.

I think maybe he just wanted me to think he did a good job. It never occurred to me that doctors might be insecure too. Just a little guy of a surgeon doing his best.

When I got home I got a phone call and I almost didn't answer because I figured it was the auto loan warranty motherfuckers who molest me every day but it was this same guy asking me how I felt and I said wait who is this again? Doctor who? Lowercase who. I had never had a doctor be interested in me for more than five seconds after I'd walked out of his room in my life. I always pictured my doctors powering down to factory settings after they were no longer in my line of sight.

But no it was him and instead it was like I went to my buddy's first concert and he called me later to ask how it went desperate for affirmation so I said uh yes you did a good job doctor buddy. It really looked like you guys were having a good time up there I said.

I started to think this guy didn't want to be my doctor he wanted to be my friend. I was going to have to check but I was pretty sure my insurance doesn't cover that.

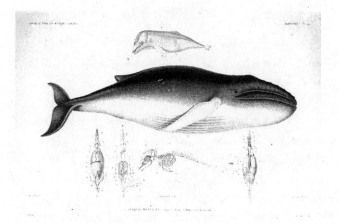

His traps never empty

There's a wall devoted to the dead in my mother's house. Some of the photos are big and some are very small from when photos had to be small by necessity and they're all mounted in ornate-looking frames although I imagine they are actually pretty cheap yard sale shit like wood painted gold.

My grandmother whose name I definitely know used to love to go to yard sales and she would bring me along sometimes and I'd dig through the weird old people's sad old shit and get depressed about it when they didn't have any comic books.

How much for this once-cherished reminder of your brief stay on Earth people would ask the yard sale lady and she would stand there on her lawn smoking a cigarette and think about it for a second and go for you I can do that today for one single quarter and the other person would go like hmm I don't know how about a nickel?

The way the photos are arranged it looks like something you would find in the drawing room of an insane magician's haunted mansion and you'd go did that one's eyes just move what the fuck? Meanwhile the magician is sneaking up behind you and he honestly believes he's invisible.

I've been thinking about it all weekend because I read something that fucked me up and made me try as hard as I can to remember the names of the people in the photos on the wall most of whom are my great-grandparents. I can't really do it and it's stressing me out.

It was a quote from this book called *The Happiness Myth* which I didn't read but I saw a screenshot of on Twitter which counts as close enough to having read a book nowadays and the writer said she had asked a bunch of people she knew how many of their four great-grandmothers they could name. Only a few knew even one or two.

"These are the mothers of people you have loved, spent days with, and possibly mourned," she wrote.

To be sure I know the names of a lot of my great-grandparents because once a year at Christmas I'll ask my parents to tell me who the people in the photos are and explain what they know about them and I'll think about them for a while like ah the rich tapestry of our shared ancestry is a marvel indeed. Then I'll have fifteen plastic cups of warm Dewars and almost instantly the information will leak out of my porous sieve-like brain and be gone until the next time when I have to ask all over again.

The guy from *Memento* except it's not my own life I forget every day it's the lives of the people who came before me.

My own life too but less so.

Worse tattoos than that also.

One of my great-grandmothers is named Nora I want to say. There's a Lillian too. A bunch of old-timey names like that that people are giving their babies again now.

I did a poll on Twitter asking how many of their eight great-grandparents' names people knew and about 2,000 responded. Forty percent said 1–2. Thirty-six percent said none.

In that passage up above from the book I didn't read the author wrote "Koheleth was right. We are not going to be remembered."

Koheleth is one of the names for "the teacher" in the book of Ecclesiastes. Some people think it's supposed to be King Solomon and other people don't think it is and who is to say certainly not me. I don't know anything and even if I did I wouldn't remember it.

He is described as a king and the son of David and the text is essentially some heavy existential shit that can be summarized thusly:

lolnothingmatters.gif

It's also written in a surprisingly ironic tone which is weird to think about. That they had irony 2,500 years ago. Then again the general point of the whole thing is that nothing about human life ever changes and it's all one long slide toward oblivion and that there is nothing new under the sun so I guess it's not weird that this fella would be any different from you and I.

That phrase nothing new under the sun is one of many things from the text that has lingered in our collective consciousness. It's also where the whole for everything there is a season and a time for every purpose under Heaven bit came from that you hear people read at funerals or in that one famous song with the pretty harmonies.

Everything we do is meaningless and life is nothing but striving after wind the guy writes. Better to have never been born he writes.

At least I think that's what he meant. Just between you and me it honestly feels sort of weird to be sitting here reading passages from the Bible on a Sunday morning like some kind of pervert.

"Meaningless! Meaningless!" says the Teacher. "Utterly meaningless! Everything is meaningless."

"What do people gain from all their labors at which they toil under the sun? Generations come and generations go, but the earth remains forever. The sun rises and the sun sets, and hurries back to where it rises. The wind blows to the south and turns to the north; round and round it goes, ever returning on its course. All streams flow into the sea, yet the sea is never full. To the place the streams come from, there they return again. All things are wearisome, more than one can say. The eye never has enough of seeing, nor the ear its fill of hearing."

The sea is never full.

"What has been will be again, what has been done will be done again; there is nothing new under the sun."

Then he goes:

"A man may have a hundred children and live many years; yet no matter how long he lives, if he cannot enjoy his prosperity and does not receive proper burial,

I say that a stillborn child is better off than he. It comes without meaning, it departs in darkness, and in darkness its name is shrouded. Though it never saw the sun or knew anything, it has more rest than does that man."

Hm.

It all sounds really bleak and nihilistic I guess but then at the end there's a conclusion tacked on which essentially says anyway that's why you gotta love God and follow all his rules or else!

I am no Bible scholar but I think maybe someone else added that part in post-production like when a really dark movie doesn't test well with audiences and the execs are like ah let's make this a little more appealing to consumers. Pep it up.

The Bible was basically a Google doc where everyone had editing permission turned on.

My mother called me back just now and told me all the names of my great-grandparents that she could rustle up and there was Maude and James and Friedrich and Lillian and Nora and Patrick.

Then she told me she recently found a toy wooden truck that someone had apparently given to me when I was a child and on the bottom of it it read from Dick Callahan, Round Pond, Maine and she said she was sad to realize she had no idea who Dick Callahan was anymore and what was even sadder than that was she said she had no one left who she could call to even ask about him as they were all dead now too. Everyone was dead.

I don't have any clue what toy truck she's talking about. I don't remember ever even having a wooden toy truck never mind who the hell this nice man Dick Callahan was.

Thank you for the truck though Mr. Callahan. I found your obituary eventually while I was writing this and it seems like you were a fella with a loving family. It said you served honorably in World War II and then worked as a well driller and at the ironworks in Bath. It said you made beautiful hooked rugs and loved woodworking. I now know more about you than any of my ancestors I named above until I get a chance to ask again next Christmas and all you ever gave me was a wooden truck unlike all of those dead people who gave me all of everything else inside of my blood.

That was a nice gesture on your behalf though and someday I'll be dead too and maybe I'll come float over to whatever the Maine section of Heaven they have up there is with the rocky cold beaches and I can thank you. Every lobsterman in Heaven Maine going out and his traps never empty.

I don't know how Heaven works maybe we'll both be men in the prime of our lives forever up there and we can shake hands and have a beer or maybe how you see it will be I'm a little boy driving a toy wooden truck around at your feet and you'll be looking around like does anyone know whose kid this is? Nora is this your great-grand kid you'll shout and she won't even remember either. Lillian?

To the ground

An ant was trekking across the porch up and over the contours of the warped boards and rusted nails and the scars where the gray paint had been chipped away over the years by wind and rain and your heavy steps. The height of it all must have seemed mountainous to the exhausted ant and sometimes when you would see a solitary scout sniffing around like that into your personal business you would hold a burning cigarette down in front of its path not to kill it or hurt it or anything but rather to give it the impression that the place it was trying to go was on fire so it would take that information back to its friends and they would know better than to come around here anymore. Like a convoluted impossible to discern signal that God would send you or I and then be mad when it didn't translate. Maybe ants don't get tired I don't know. When it's expected of you to work yourself to death maybe exhaustion isn't even a concept.

PTEROMYS LEPIDUS.

London, Published by Henry G. Bohn, York Street, Covent Garden, 1833

Last card in the shoe

There had been a particularly bad leak at the processing plant one night just over there the guy was telling me. He gestured out to where I was supposed to picture rows of factories but it was a baseball field now and just a couple of leftover smoke stacks behind it.

Everyone was woken up in the middle of the night gasping for air he said. If you were out driving you would have had to pull over so you wouldn't crash like in a snow squall but in this case it was a storm of poison.

That sort of thing wasn't all that uncommon back then he said.

That's fucked up I said.

Yeah it was fucked up he said.

Along the river here was where all the big chemical companies had their plants for a hundred years and they'd spit the gas into the sky and dump the runoff into the water and bury anything else under the dirt. Since they were some of the biggest employers in the state the politicians looked the other way and the people largely took it because what choice did they have. All the workers lived nearby and got used to the belching smoke and acid leaks like it was the weather changing.

He asked me for a cigarette there on the deck of the casino and I gave him one and looked out at the one single wind turbine over there rotating and doing its best. Someone should write a book about windmills and futility.

I sometimes thought that it's weird that the city's unofficial song is the one about loving the polluted water. That band wasn't even from here. A band from Los Angeles writing a song about how bad Boston sucks and we're still singing it sixty years later.

The water isn't as bad as it used to be now they say. They even have one day a year where people go swimming in the Charles and the news makes a whole thing about it.

When I walk down along the river on this pretty little stretch underneath the elegantly draping trees lining the path it all looks so pretty. The rowers are there setting off on their longboats and their long lives and it is very picturesque indeed the type of thing you'd put on the cover of an expensive university brochure to lure people in. The thing is it smells so bad it's almost not worth the view. I thought for a while it was all the goose shit everywhere but now I think the proximate earth just smells like that and there's no fixing it.

This goose I saw the other day down by the river though. It was motionless in the grass with its head turned inward on its plump body and deathly still. I couldn't be sure if it was suffering or merely resting. The difference is often imperceptible.

When someone dies people always say ah you don't like to see it but alas they're resting now and I guess so but the point of rest is to rejuvenate you for later.

Maybe everyone who ever died in history is napping right now for a busy night they have coming up soon.

Wait did I just invent Christianity?

Way back in the 1800s this particular stretch of waterfront that we were looking out at was owned by a man who opened what is now the oldest continuously operating restaurant in the country. You could go there right now and eat local oysters if you wanted to although to be clear they shouldn't be too local. You wouldn't want to try those I don't think. Eat local within reason.

Every night right after supper the steam would come and our eyes would water the guy said. I don't remember what he looked like anymore. He looked like you're imagining he does. A Celtics hoodie on. Cigarette face. He looked like I do but a few steps further along in the evolution.

There was a Sinatra song playing from a speaker hidden inside some architectured landscaping because he's still synonymous with casinos even now somehow.

Before they built this place they had to ship out hundreds of thousands of tons of contaminated earth the guy said. Hundreds of thousands of tons. Arsenic and lead and asbestos and what not.

Wait do you work here or something I asked and he said no.

Where did they bring it?

I don't know. New Hampshire probably.

That's fair I said.

Earlier when I had driven here in standstill traffic listening to the game I passed by a defunct tanning oils textile building with the lettering faded into the side of the brick. Across the street from there was a power station that mostly burns natural gas a lot of which comes from a country where our war planes are being used to bomb civilians to death. Not by us though so it technically is fine. It doesn't count as us doing it.

Nearer still to the luxury resort there was a sign out in front of a shop that said we buy scrap metal/cash for gold.

Every casino I've ever been to is depressing in its own way but none of them have anything on the surrounding neighborhoods.

I said well alright man nice to meet you to the guy and stepped on my cigarette on the patio and went inside and right there was a giant piece of shit garish statue of Popeye made by the famous casino artist that they had bought for like $30 million. People were standing by it getting their picture taken doing like a Popeye type of thing with their arms. After he'd eaten the spinach.

I used to have a little bit of trouble with gambling years back. Nothing crazy but enough that it was like wait a minute. In college a group of us would often drive down to the closest casino in the woods and spend whatever money we could scrape together playing blackjack and ideally stretch it out into a whole night if we could. We had a rich friend who we used to bully into lending us money to play with sometimes and I feel bad about that looking back on it but now he's a big plastic surgeon and I'm whatever I am so maybe he had it coming.

I used to think it was the coolest thing in the world to be at a casino then but more likely what I was experiencing was just how it's cool to be anywhere when you're twenty-one.

The old ladies in wheelchairs with oxygen tanks would pull the levers on the slot machines and the grumpy Asian tourists would sit silently at the tables cursing their luck and the scary guys with their tall girlfriends wobbling behind them in their high heels and eyelashes would go all in angrily and I'd lose my $75 or whatever and be like ah well that sucks but I still have my whole life in front of me. At least I have that to look forward to.

Even though it had been years being inside a casino again was making my brain maggots wriggle. I found a $25 blackjack table and sat down for about twenty minutes working to get high. It was like trying to rekindle an old flame. Mostly I just drank now to feel the same thing gambling used to make me feel which was hollowed out. A person spends so much time trying to stay in control it was a mercy to become a ragdoll in a washing machine for a cycle again.

If you've ever spent any time in a casino you might know the feeling of chasing. You keep putting your chips in thinking something is going to change. Maybe you win a hand and your spirits are briefly buoyed but it doesn't last. The reason you sat down in the first place even if you don't know it or aren't ready to admit it to yourself is that you wanted to lose. The voracious house is more than happy to oblige you in that endeavor.

It's like one of those weirdos you read about every now and again who offer themselves up to be eaten by a cannibal.

That's what drinking or using does too and it costs a lot less money-wise. The first sip is a roll of the dice or a shuffle of the cards and part of the excitement is in finding out what's going to happen next even if you know logically that the odds are it's going to a bummer. Let's find out anyway though. Are you going to be lifted albeit briefly into a euphoria you spend the rest of the night trying to catch up to or are you instead pouring yourself a cup of anger or shame or sadness. Sometimes all of those at once.

As they were digging down into the dirt on the site of the casino before construction to see how fucked they were environmentally speaking they uncovered all sorts of secrets like evidence of old facilities and plants that had simply been bulldozed over and buried in order to build new ones on top of sometimes with the chemicals they produced not even disposed of in any way. They just let the poison sink in.

That time I saw the big dead but actually alive goose I called Animal Control and they didn't answer so I called the cops next and told them there was a big dead goose on the sidewalk and could anyone do anything then I felt weird about calling the cops on a bird. The next day I went by again and it was sitting there in the exact same spot as alive as anything has ever been alive and I was glad for once that the cops don't do anything when you ask them for help.

I lost a few hands then lost again and got up to leave because I wasn't interested anymore in getting sucked back into desperation and I looked up and noticed there were all these big lobster-red chandeliers hanging over the gaming floor and I couldn't escape the feeling that I was inside of a claw grab game at an arcade waiting to be plucked out. I was a cheap stuffed animal stitched by a seven-year-old across the world that some other powerful indifferent child in the sky whoever you want it to be was aiming the grabber at and it kept reaching down just almost catching me like ah shit shit almost and they had to keep trying again and again until eventually it worked and I got pulled out and I was gone.

If you were lucky the thing dropped you at the last second. Just when the god child thought it had your ass.

I left and went down into the garage and got into my car and turned on the radio and listened to the rest of the game and the fucking bums were losing. I traced the same path in reverse but in less traffic now and headed toward home following the highway along the river the entire way. There were kids out rowing putting everything they had into it. I was never going to try that hard to do anything ever again.

There are two types of anxiety when it comes to addicts.

There is the anxiety of waiting for the drugs to arrive and there is the anxiety of realizing that the drugs are about to run out. Sometimes in between there is the high of being on the drugs but that is fleeting. That's what people inside a casino all look like. They're waiting for something to arrive and watching it run out at the same time. They just want it all to be over with whatever it's going to be.

THRESHER

Extraordinary Popular Delusions

Two planes fell from the sky killing everyone aboard and the next day they dragged the president of the plane company in front of a panel of assholes to ask what had happened and he said the computer was totally fucked and after that they let him go and retire and collect millions of dollars in benefits he was owed which is called a golden parachute. I never liked that term. If you tried to jump out of a plane with a parachute made of gold you would fall so much faster than normal as far as my understanding of physics goes which is very limited. Gold is very heavy that's like one thing about gold we all know.

Down the street from the conference two policemen posed for a photo with a bunch of cardboard signs they had stolen from a person living on the street and in the photo they are grinning real big like a policeman grins with his whole body like a nothing bad will ever happen to me type of grin.

All the signs they had taken say the same thing which is need help thank you god bless and they're holding the signs with those big arms that cops have now like rocks in a loose sock the cop muscles which seem unnecessary to me because you don't have to be particularly strong to shoot someone in the back while they're running away.

At least twenty-five people are dead after a boat fire off the coast of Maine and at least five people are dead after a hurricane pummeled Connecticut and seven people are dead and twenty-two more are wounded after a shooting in Pennsylvania no not that one a new one and you can turn on your TV right now and watch them all being talked about one after the other if you want just flip back and forth from one channel to the next and it's like a scene in a disaster movie where the person is watching TV in the background to let you know things are going to all hell. They flip channel by channel and weirdly even now in movies they still do this as like a stylistic choice they make it so the channel changing has that old percussive chunking sound where you'd hear a bit of static in the spaces in between. TVs don't do that anymore they don't make that sound anymore the toggling between everything is a lot more seamless and streamlined now.

Love will save you

The famous swans were back and so they walked along the bike path to where the river opened up downstream from the mill to go take pictures of them. So they could let other people know they had seen a swan family once. The kids were all riled up about it and you had to lean into that whenever you got the chance. To get them invested in nature.

As they came up on the bridge they saw a few other groups taking their own pictures and then a bunny darted by their feet as if it were being chased by something into the woods.

The kids had been bugging them lately about getting a pet of some kind but that was more of a we'll see type of situation. Everyone knew who would be responsible for the cleaning up after it about two weeks into the whole thing.

Did you ever have a bunny?

Stickers she said.

Stickers was a white rabbit with beautiful brown and caramel-brown marks and I thought the marks looked like stickers so I named it Stickers she said.

How old were you?

I was probably like seven.

You had a rabbit hutch and everything?

Yeah. In the woods. You know how far away the woods are from the house? You had to walk clear out. I don't know why we didn't put it closer.

Did you go and see them all that much?

Like every day. But that's what I've been telling you about pets. The mountains of shit would pile up. Tiny little round turds. Mountains of little round turds. Then in the winter they would freeze and you would have to literally scrape the shit off. I didn't do it but I just have it in my mind. My mom she was the only one who would do it. Obviously. It's obvious she was the only one who did it.

The boy had climbed up onto the railing of the bridge and was waving his arms above his head like he was trying to signal to the swans to come closer.

He worried sometimes that the boy was going to be some kind of asshole when he grew up which is one of the few possible outcomes. It's either that or they end up as some nerd which is the best-case scenario or else just some random guy.

There were two bunnies she said. I was seven when they ran away. Yes seven. I remember I had them in kindergarten. The reason I know is I had a very traumatic experience that I still remember. I was in kindergarten in Mrs. Bayman's class. We got to all have a special share day. I was so excited to bring my bunny in for share day. So I brought Stickers. I have no idea how this was facilitated. My mom probably drove Stickers in. I don't know if she was in the room or if she was there when this happened but we were all sitting in the share circle and I reached into whatever sort of travel case it was to procure Stickers to show everyone. Here's my bunny! The kids were obviously very excited.

And Stickers absolutely freaked the fuck out. On me. I was holding Stickers and she clawed me. Scratched me up. I kept holding her because I was afraid she was going to escape. She scratched the shit out of me then leapt out of my hand. I don't even know what happened next.

You don't even know how excited a kindergartener was to bring their bunny to school. I was that excited. Then Stickers attacked me in front of all my friends. I was crying inconsolably. Someone had to walk me to the nurse and I had to get all bandaged up. I was so embarrassed. Humiliated. I don't even know . . . I don't know who caught Stickers or what happened to Stickers after that. All I know is I went from being like this is the best day of my life to being so humiliated.

Poor baby he said. What happened to it later?

That day?

No later.

Stickers was probably new that year. The other one I just want you to know had the most annoying name but my brother named it. I don't think anyone in my family said the name right. We called the bunny Nub-you-noy. My brother thought of the name and it was supposed to be Honeybun backwards. If you say Honeybun backwards it does not say oy at the end it's oh. It starts with ho so it's going to end with oh. So we thought it was so smart and we were sitting here mispronouncing it our whole lives.

Well kids are very dumb.

My parents called it that too! I'm pretty sure my uncle built the hutch. Oh my poor uncle. I don't know how long we had them. Two maybe three years. We 100 percent lost interest in them so my mom would have to go out and shovel the mounds of shit. But then they escaped. Looking back I'm thinking maybe someone let them out. I don't know that anybody would do that.

Maybe your mom wanted a break?

I don't think she would do that. But they disappeared into the night. Never to be seen again.

Did you cry?

Yeah I was wicked sad. Do you know how much I loved animals? I loved animals so much when I was little.

You had an imaginary horse!

Yeah! I loved animals. When I got my first Communion and you get all the money . . . Did you do that?

Yeah I got some money.

I remember I got all this cash. I remember sitting my mom down in second grade saying I know what I want to do with my money and she was like what and I said I want a cat. She said no and I cried so hard. I always wanted a cat.

You've never had a cat as long as I've known you.

We had so many cats when I was growing up! We had like eight cats. But they would always die because they were never indoor cats. You know Ozzy right?

No I only remember Razor the dog.

Ozzy was my cat. I never told you Ozzy stories? After my First Communion my mom brought me to the seed and feed store. A very famous store. They would have kittens there. I don't know if they were for sale. I think they were free. I would always want to go with my mom to the seed and feed store to see the kittens. So I went with her and we were in there and she was like do you want one? I said yeah! She said you can take one. It can be yours. There was a very adorable little kitten that was rascally and fighting and there was a bigger gray striped cat that was purring and cuddling like there's no tomorrow. I debated it and I said I don't know this one seems really sweet but I want a kitten and my mom said they're all gonna grow up eventually so if you think that one has the cutest personality you should get that one. So I did and Ozzy was a total maniac. I 100 percent named him Ozzy to impress my older siblings. He lived up to his name.

Crazy Train.

Yeah he was Crazy Train. I had friends who were literally afraid to sleep over because of Ozzy.

So Ozzy died from a raccoon fight. That was a very sad story. He was an outdoor cat and he was like a hunter. One night he brought us a bunny. He came to the door and we let him in and he just spat out this baby bunny right on the floor. It was so adorable but its stomach was all gashed open by Ozzy. Me and my mom put Neosporin on its stomach and gave it water and food and put it in a little box in the basement to keep it safe from Ozzy. I was so excited because this was after the bunnies had run away. I was like if it lives can I keep it as a pet and my mom was like we'll see.

I went to bed so excited and I woke up the next morning and said how's the bunny and my mom said the bunny is dead.

Fucking Ozzy he said.

But Ozzy died from fighting with a racoon one night. It was a summer night. He came home in the middle of the night. My mom and I were the only ones awake. He was gashed open now.

The raccoon got his ass?

The racoon got his ass. Someone finally got Ozzy's ass. He was a real hunter. We brought him to the emergency vet. I don't know what town it was in. They were like you need to quarantine this cat for three months. It cannot be around any other animal. If you can't do that you need to put him down right now. We were traumatized because we knew Ozzy. He could not be inside. He had to be outside. He would always climb the screens trying to get out. My mom being the honest person that she is was like we can't guarantee we're going to keep him inside for three months. It's not possible. And the woman was like we need to put him down. And they put him down. Me and my mom were sobbing. We were so sad. Then we told our normal vet and he was pissed off. He said that would have never happened if you brought the cat to me. This woman murdered our cat!

They were laughing about it now but he gave her a hug anyway just in case and they stood there watching the kids yelling out to the swans to swim closer as if they could understand English. He got scared for a second about what would happen if they fell into the water. If he'd have time to save them both.

1. RANA ESCULENTA.   2. R. TEMPORARIA.   3. 4. R. RUGOSA.   5. 6. HYLA ARBOREA.   7. 8. H. HÜBNERI.

After a while your body rebels

It's all to do with the feminization of the American male the old fella said nakedly.

Uh is that it I said near naked myself.

He asked me if he knew me from somewhere and I said I used to come here a lot.

No that's not you he said.

The other day in the new pool I go to now a guy in the lane next to me asked if I was me and I had to think about it for a second. Every time that happens I wonder if it's someone who's going to say something nice or if this is the time I'm finally going to get my asshole ripped off.

What do you do the old guy asked.

I'm a writer too he said still naked. Here we go I thought. I write love stories he said and I did not ask any follow-up questions about that because this guy's love stories are not my business. I hope everyone in them ends up very happy though.

I was in my old neighborhood for the day and I figured I'd go back to the YMCA for old time's sake but mostly to see if it would shake something out of me or make me sad in some sort of different more interesting way than the repetitive one I'd become accustomed to from sitting at home hiding from the sickness which does not interest even me anymore and it's my own whole thing. I've had very little interiority the past few months and zero epiphanies or revelations of any kind. I've mostly been reduced to my base animalistic impulses which are I'm in pain or I'm hungry or I'm tired or I'm horny or I'm going to dig a series of tunnels under the yard with various exit holes strewn about to more easily escape predators.

That reminds me of the chipmunk infestation I'm dealing with.

There are so many bunnies and squirrels and birds and chipmunks and shit in my yard and whenever one turns up and before they see me or sense me moving I try to get my phone out to snap a picture just in case they end up doing something silly and I guess that must be what it's like following Ben Affleck around.

Lately I mostly feel the physical pain part though. When you're in pain all the time nothing else is real and you'll take anything you can to make it stop for a few hours even if it's probably going to make things worse later on such as a bottle of alcohol.

I've been watching this show *Feel Good* and it's funny and charming if a bit predictable in its romantic comedy beats. Mae Martin plays an addict in the show and the stories are taken from their own real-life experience I understand. In the one I watched last night there's a scene with the guy who leads a recovery group and he's talking to them after they have fucked up big time.

I don't know why I did it Mae says and the guy goes "the question I would encourage you to ask is not why did I use we all know why we use. Pain relief. Instead ask yourself why the pain?"

My therapist used to be right up the road from the pool and I thought about popping back in to say hello but then I realized that's something a crazy person would do. On the other hand where better to do something crazy than therapy.

The YMCA was emptier than I ever remember it being all those years I came here. There used to be so many old people meandering around in here like this guy with the takes on masculinity just very slowly toweling off their old bodies all over the place or very slowly swimming back and forth in the pool. Maybe I just came at a dead time during the day or maybe a lot of them went ahead and actually died from the thing.

I thought it was going to be a much more emotionally resonant experience than it was this kind of homecoming but I was just a guy putting his bathing suit on and there's not much pathos in that no matter how you try to frame it.

To be fair I was probably forcing the whole thing. It's like when you're single and you want to meet someone really badly and you try and try but the desperation is palpable and so it doesn't come until you finally stop looking and then voila love finds you. The metaphors have to sneak up on you when you're busy doing other things.

For some reason I told the guy what I write about typically I said uh . . . you know health care abuses and police violence and things like that and then he told me he used to be a cop well not a cop cop but military police on a base in Albuquerque and it's a similar type of thing he said and then he wanted to tell me about some Chris Rock joke that he liked about black people and police and I was like uh oh.

Mercifully he didn't do the bit or even indicate which one it was but I just looked online after and maybe it was the one about how cops might start to think they should shoot more white kids every now and again to balance things out. So it doesn't look so obvious.

Then the guy said Joe Biden is trying to get them to put the Boston Marathon bomber to death and he was in favor of that.

I didn't say anything and sort of started looking at my phone the way you do to broadcast that you are done talking to someone and I saw a tweet that said Ringo and Shelley Duvall were an item for a while and there's a cute photo of them smiling.

You don't hear too much about Shelley Duvall these days.

I read something once about her experience filming *The Shining* and I guess Kubrick was pretty hard on her. Dozens of takes and so on and she'd have to put on sad music before each scene to get herself appropriately emotional.

The trick was you just think about something very sad in your life or how much you miss your family or friends she told an interviewer. But after a while your body rebels. It says stop doing this to me. I don't want to cry every day. And sometimes just that thought alone would make me cry.

The thing is now that they have women cops the old fella said and that screws up a man's sense of his own masculinity. So that's why they shoot to kill so quickly these days he said. They didn't used to do that.

Ok I said.

They used to shoot to uh . . . what's the word? he said.

Neutralize?

No. Disable he said.

I said well at the very least I think if you are a hard-ass cop like most of them purport to be you should be able to apprehend someone without killing them you could use some single other tactic besides instant death and he said something else about women cops and then I snapped my lock on the locker and as I was doing it I said to myself nooooooo . . . wait! like someone was shutting a cell door on me and that's when I learned the lesson that if you haven't used your gym lock in over a year make sure you check if you remember the combination beforehand. Goddamnit I said and then I remembered for some reason that I never listened to that Fiona Apple album everyone was very excited about last year or whenever that was.

Then I was thinking about how the video for "Criminal" which came out in 1997 was my version of Puberty 2. Puberty 1 is just regular puberty that we've all heard of but Puberty 2 is when your brain unlocks what kind of pervert you're going to turn into.

I stood there trying combination after combination trying to get the fucking thing unlocked and I couldn't do it. I couldn't get back inside. All I could remember was that two of the numbers were very close to one another. I could feel in my muscle memory the exact amount of distance my wrist was supposed to turn but not from where and to where.

I watched a movie the other night called *Coherence*. It was a cheaply made indie film from 2014 about a group of friends attending a dinner party in Los Angeles on the night that a mysterious comet is passing over the earth. The influence of the comet fucks with reality in such and such a way that multiple dimensions all converge in that one neighborhood for the duration of its passing. Or something. Slowly the characters realize there are other versions of themselves from slightly different realities all colliding into one another and as you can imagine that fucks with everyone's brains real good. In all the versions we see on screen the friends all resort to acting like they always were going to act. In the end the final girl tries to break free and only makes things worse for herself. She ends up in a reality that she did not begin in but seemed better than the one she was escaping from and now there were two or more of her there.

I haven't been able to stop thinking about that. What if you side-stepped into a dimension that was almost exactly like your life save for a few differences but there was someone else there that was already inhabiting your place? Somehow there being two of you feels so much more lonely than you would think. The memories you share with this alternate version of your loved ones might have similarities but they are not the people you actually love. You would think maybe you could befriend yourself or at the very least suck yourself off but I don't think it would work out that way. You'd have to kill the other version of yourself to survive.

While I was swimming I decided I would go inside my mind cavern and unlock the secret lock combination through sheer will power and logic like a somehow even stupider version of *Sherlock*. I got distracted and thought about a Cape Cod lobsterman who had recently gotten himself swallowed and spit out by a whale and had that little scary thrill like when you were a kid and convinced yourself there could be a shark below you in the pool. I thought at first it must be horrific beyond measure to be swallowed by a whale but then I realized it wouldn't be much different than dying any other way in the long run. Something is going to swallow you and it will get dark and terrifying it's just a matter of how long it takes for you to go under.

My friend told me he has a dream about being back in high school and never being able to remember the combination to his locker and I said oh my god I have that one all the time too and now I don't know for sure if that's true or if he just implanted that memory into my brain by saying it. The sense that there's something so important inside of there just out of reach that you desperately need access to and no matter how many variations of the same pattern you try and try and try you just can't get to where you need to be.

My whole life I've never seen anything like it

The March Against Death began on a Thursday night fifty-three years ago today at Arlington National Cemetery where they make the graves very handsome.

There are roughly 400,000 ugly bodies in the handsome graves there and fifty-three years ago at least that many living bodies marched on DC that weekend in a series of protests because the dead weren't available to march for themselves they were otherwise engaged.

This is unrelated but I just thought of a scene in the *Watchmen* TV show where the main guy is making breakfast for his young children and one of them asks where their uncle figure who was killed is now and the guy goes before he was born he was nowhere and now he's nowhere again.

Then he made waffles and the kids got invested in that.

Many of the protesters on that Thursday in DC carried signs with the names of people who had killed and been killed in Vietnam and would perhaps have their bones shipped all the way back to the famous cemetery before all was said and done. There was a lot more killing and being killed to do as it was only 1969 and it wouldn't all stop for another four to six years depending on how you tabulate the accumulation of bodies.

Wait maybe *Watchmen* is related because the Vietnam War plays a big role in the plot of the comic book.

I think about the Vietnam War sometimes and it seems as distant in history as the invention of the automobile to my life but it wasn't. I was almost starting to be born a year or two or three or four or five after the last person was killing or being killed there. My mother was a teenager and she was almost ready to have her second baby but this one she would get to hold for more than 60 seconds before the nurses' mood changed.

They say almost 60,000 of our brave heroic soldiers died over there and people always say we lost that war but around two million Vietnamese died too so I don't know what it really means to lose under that type of accounting.

Some of the signs the marchers carried also had the names of villages that had been destroyed.

It was cold that day in 1969 and when the protesters marched single file from Arlington across the bridge to the White House they were bundled up pretty good and as they passed the fence around the president's house they paused and yelled out a name of the dead. Some of them were quiet and timid in doing so and some of them were so angry their voices were hoarse and their bodies shook.

The Mỹ Lai massacre had recently been exposed around then and people weren't very happy about that as you might imagine. We used our helicopter guns against kids.

I understand obviously why machine-gunning civilians to death is worse than machine-gunning "the enemy" to death and I guess the thinking behind that is the civilians aren't capable of or actively trying to hurt "us" and so there is no justification to slaughter them but I never understand why the people who draw that line don't also extrapolate it out to its inevitable widening conclusion when it comes to starting the wars in the first place.

"My conscience won't let me go shoot my brother, or some darker people, or some poor hungry people in the mud for big powerful America," Muhammad Ali said around 1967 on his refusal to enlist.

"And shoot them for what?"

Elsewhere in the country some of the parents of those who killed and were killed in Vietnam tried to bar the protest group from speaking the names of their dead children.

They didn't like the idea of their children being used for politics.

One by one each of the protesters deposited their signs with the names of the dead into prop coffins they had set up and Nixon was up late into the night watching it all unfold on TV like a sweaty pervert. I was going to say but thankfully now he's in Hell with the rest of our presidents but the truth is he's nowhere.

Nothing particularly violent happened that weekend. At least not in DC anyway. Lots of violent things happened in Vietnam. As the protest grew into the hundreds of thousands the military and the police were standing by with many of them hiding out of sight in case they had to ambush what must have seemed like an occupying force. It's got to fucking suck to have your city invaded I would imagine.

I'm pretty sure the whole thing about protesters spitting on soldiers when they came back from Vietnam was made up or else greatly exaggerated but if it did happen I bet they all would have much preferred to spit on Nixon they just didn't have a good sight on him which is exactly how war works. You have to shoot whoever is closest and it's never the main bad guys.

Nixon was asked a few weeks earlier whether or not anyone from the burgeoning protest movement had convinced him to reconsider the war and he said lol no it's just the hippies on college campuses he said. It's not real people. He said it was basically no big deal. Thankfully our leaders don't treat the left like that anymore.

I read a newspaper story where some people were quoted saying the protesters were all enemies of freedom and so on. You can probably imagine what they said verbatim on your own. It's funny to think that the Boomers had Boomers of their own who hated them all the same.

On Saturday of that weekend in 1969 around 500,000 gathered across from the White House and lots of performers were there like Pete Seeger and John Denver and Arlo Guthrie and they all sang "Give Peace a Chance" etcetera and maybe it worked I don't know but around that same time Nixon was escalating our project of carpet bombing the unmerciful shit out of Cambodia and that would go on for a few more years.

Four students at Kent State were murdered by the Ohio National Guard in May of 1970 during protests against that bombing campaign. Neil Young wrote a song about that shooting which you know I'm sure.

One time I was walking across the bridge from Georgetown to Arlington with a girl I had just started seeing. It would have been around 1998. I don't remember much about the date in question except that we probably had something for dinner that didn't agree with me because halfway across I was paralyzed by sudden onset diarrhea poisoning. There aren't many hard and fast rules about the mating rituals of young humans but I am fairly certain one of them is don't shit your pants in front of the other person and so I smuggled this dark secret of my bowels and its boiling stew across the bridge marching as stoically as I could manage and after what seemed like ten miles a McDonald's appeared in the distance like an oasis for a guy crawling in the desert and I hustled inside and as I was opening the door to the stall of the bathroom and pulling my pants down in one smooth motion I sprayed a torrent of shit all over the wall like a firefighter who lost control of his hose. Then it was out of me and I felt better. I tried to clean up as best I could but I don't think I did a good enough job so I am sorry to whoever was working at that McDonald's that night if you're reading this.

On my phone just now I saw a nice bowl of moules-frites and a drone photo a guy took of his wife lying on the beach in Puerto Rico and some foliage in Massachusetts and a pop star in lingerie riding a mechanical bull and a rum cocktail someone had poured into a hollowed-out gourd and a sunset on the Florida Keys and the shadow of a figure in the tall grass on a gray marsh and the charred remains of a car destroyed by a fire and an ad for knives and an ad for pants and an ad for sneakers and an ad for blazers and a dancing robot dog with a machine gun on its back and somebody's dead grandfather and everybody's dead David Bowie and I thought about how it was all supposed to make me covetous of something I don't have and then I saw someone in Costa Rica posted a series of videos of some hatchling turtles or tortoises I don't know the difference and they were crawling out of a hole in the sand confused and blinking in the red light.

Some of them struck out instantly for the ocean instinctively and some lingered and reached out with their flippers to pull the next one close for safety and didn't seem to know what direction they were meant to go.

My uncle who was married to one of my dead father's dead sisters was in Vietnam but I don't know him anymore. He gave me a POW/MIA sticker that I put in my bedroom window when I was a child. I didn't really understand what the concept meant but I remember Rambo was especially sore about it.

The other day I was talking to my other living father and he told me his dog had died that week. He had rushed her to the animal hospital and they couldn't save her and he was fucked up about it. He told me whenever he took the dogs walking and running on the fields near the high school where I used to play sports that all the kids would know the dogs and pat them and stuff and I think he was proud that the local student athletes knew who his dogs were.

Then we talked about a high school classmate of mine who had died the day before from an overdose and her husband who had died from an overdose a couple years earlier. My friend who is a firefighter in the town I grew up in said he was on the call to her house the night she died and one of her little daughters was asking him why they weren't rushing her mother to the hospital the whole time but I'm sure you can figure out why.

My niece had been over at the house hanging out the day before she died and her friend texted her the next day "mom is dead."

Something about how she didn't text "my mom" is fucking me up. Just lowercase "mom." Of course that wouldn't refer to anyone else in her experience.

Then my living father told me he was doing fine with his leukemia and from the way he tells it he has some sort of luxury leukemia that is basically nothing. I used to freak out about it when he first got it but now I barely even remember he has it. Then he joked about me dying young. Didn't all your aunts and father die at sixty he said and I said I think so. He told me about when one of my dead aunts was on her deathbed. Her sister went to try to make amends and the first aunt was basically like no fuck you too late for that and she wouldn't see her and then she died and then not too long after the other one died and then not too long after that me and everyone reading this died.

I don't know if this is just a Massachusetts Irish thing but a weird part of getting older is finding out just how many of the people who used to watch you open Christmas presents went on to hate each other's fucking guts.

The last time I saw that aunt she was in a coffin. I hugged her daughters who I was very close to growing up but don't really see any more and then the next time I saw them it was at the funeral of one of their husbands who died from an overdose a couple years ago.

This is how you know this piece is kind of barely disguised non-fiction because if you made up so many overdoses in a row in a short story it would seem fake but not so in real life.

I haven't seen any of them since then but probably will at the next funeral. Maybe when I overdose.

I don't know what type of music any of those people I mentioned just now like or liked besides my living father. He likes Neil Young pretty good I think and sometimes he plays "Old Man" on the piano. I think he likes Van Morrison the best. At one point he must have liked Arlo Guthrie who was at that protest in DC because the first dog of ours I remember loving was an Irish Setter named Arlo and when he died I got pretty fucked up about it. Sometimes he'll learn like an Oasis or Goo Goo Dolls song or something from the nineties where I am from and play it for me maybe to bond with me and I get the guitar and sing with him but that doesn't happen as often as it used to anymore.

The last time I saw his mother alive we wheeled her down into the basement of the nursing facility where there was a piano and he played some songs for her while she sat there but I don't know if she knew anything about it or anything at all.

Toward the end she would confuse him for her husband who had been dead for like twenty years and he would bust her balls about it like joking around pretending to be him and my mom would have to be like hey cut that out.

Everyone has read *The Things They Carried* the famous book of stories about Vietnam by Tim O'Brien.

I haven't read it in twenty years or more maybe. Not since that grandfather I just mentioned was alive. I was reminded of it earlier this week when it was Veterans Day.

Even though O'Brien's book was one of the most impactful collections of short stories I have ever read in my life it's been so long since I've read it I don't remember many details besides one which is the scene where the guy shoots a water buffalo to pieces bit by bit. He shoots it in the knee then the mouth then the tail and so on but it just won't die and the rest of the platoon watches him doing it and are like what the fuck is this guy's deal but they know because it was their deal too.

I remembered this morning that I remembered that scene and you probably do too and I was embarrassed in a way because it's such a big dangling meatball of a metaphor about mankind's cruelty and indifference to life like it's the scene that's supposed to punch you in the gut but it seems silly that it takes the systematic disinterested and casual slaughter of a dumb brute beast to drive the point home that killing is bad.

Why did I only remember the water buffalo dying of all the things in that book?

The first thing I could think of is that we think that in war the people on the other side are supposed to die and that is the natural order of things but the animal didn't do anything to deserve its violent death.

I'm not sure why we don't also extrapolate that out to its inevitable conclusion when it comes to starting wars in the first place.

I looked at my phone again and I saw a lineup of daiquiri shots on a brass bar that I've sat at too many times to count and a series of photos and videos of a young mother's baby either a boy or girl I don't know the difference and it was crawling around in the grass confused and blinking in the new sun and didn't seem to know what direction it was meant to go and a bunch of troops sitting on a tank with the caption thank you for your service. Then I saw a football player had posted a series of photos of himself shaking hands with troops in various types of troop hats and a fancy hotel in Newport Rhode Island I stayed in one time offering a holiday special and the gang from the funny improv podcast yucking it up and a sad bowl of miso soup and Rod Stewart looking fashionable in a coat and another photo from the Florida Keys of some scuba divers unfurling a giant American flag underwater at the site of a sunken navy ship at a place I have snorkeled at.

Home of the free because of the brave the caption on the photo read and the flag is billowing out from the focal point of the camera like an enormous poisonous jellyfish and the guys yanking it along all look so proud. They have diving masks on but you can still tell they're smiling and really happy about what they did here.

I want to see you dance again

What is that she said and he didn't immediately answer so she said it again. What is that she said this time like a drum beat what is that kick snare crash and not comprehending the words themselves but nonetheless sensing the urgency of the tone like a dog can do he stood up and walked to the foot of the staircase and said hwwuha and she said come look at this and so he made his way to go look at it.

Just a minute before he had been swiping through a series of videos of birds that could mimic human language and each was more enchanting than the last. The type of thing where you'd go haha babe you gotta see this or text it to her so she'd think you were kindly and the bird is going like I'm Mr. Food Man and I love God's Pure Light in that adorable uncanny way they can feint speech and therefore approximate a sort of imprisoned humanity. As if reporting the news from the bottom of a well.

In the last video he watched a crow was sitting there in a cage unable to fly or leave or do anything a bird needs to do to realize its birdhood and it goes Hi Joe.

Hi Joe.

You'd have to guess Joe must have been the fella taking the video.

Then the bird goes The Hangman is coming.

The Hangman is coming.

It looks into the camera like it's staring right at you personally and just one more time for the road it goes The Hangman is coming in its tongueless bird tongue and the video ends after that.

The video was short so it never tied off the arc of whether or not the Hangman showed up. Eventually he will have made his way over there for Joe and the bird and everywhere else for every breathing creature you can only assume given how time and his job description works.

Hi Joe. The Hangman is coming.

Wait do birds have tongues or not?

Most of the birds you see in videos like that don't say that type of shit. They usually go pee pee momma and that sort of thing. We're a little baby boy and we wanted the worm for our mouth.

Give us the little worm for our mouth momma.

Then there was a news story about a five month old bar-tailed godwit that had been tagged and was tracked flying 8,435 miles nonstop from Alaska to Australia in a trip that took 11 days straight in the air and all of a sudden some other bird being able to give voice to a disembodied spirit wasn't quite so impressive anymore. All birds are capable of summoning the eldritch but not all of them are fucking jacked.

What is that she said using her phone's flashlight like a private investigator with a comic book magnifying glass and having summeted and now standing there alongside he said I don't think it's anything. It looks like a mouse turd maybe.

How would a mouse shit up that high?

A dead little . . . moth larva maybe he said not knowing how he knew what the different strata of larvae were or if strata was the right word to disentangle them from one another species wise.

Look closer she said and he said baby it's nothing let's not do this right now ok baby? Being kind of a prick about it and then feeling bad five seconds later but it was too late to turn back. How the quality of the word baby can disintegrate in your mouth in the short duration of any sentence it bookends. He looked closer anyway and one of the tiny little maggots (?) was convulsing with the rhythm of his heartbeat one two three one two three one two three like skeletons waltzing and as a reflex he flicked it to Hell which was the wrong thing to do for numerous reasons.

Why did you do that?

I don't know!

Now I have to find it again.

I'm sorry I'll call a guy tomorrow.

He left her to her inspections and walked slowly left hand braced back down the stairs with his other arm cocking at the ready like a pugnacious cowboy itching for his holster and had the phone out in motion smoothing felicity as he flopped onto the couch and a moment later there for his eyeballs was a story about an immigrant who had died by suicide in a New York prison. The guard in his cell block had lied about having checked on him regularly the story said and in the interim the guy had scrawled on the wall a note.

Perdi mi memoria. No recuerdo nada he wrote.

I lost my memory completely. I don't remember anything.

I leave you free he wrote.

The story said the man had had some sort of accident years ago some sort of trauma to the skull and hadn't been the same since and had resorted to alcoholism to cope with that which is a very understandable response to trauma of any kind.

On another part of the wall he had also written mi esposa los amor and you can probably understand the bulk of the meaning there even if you don't speak his language.

He swiped away from all of that and saw that Paul Verhoeven's Starship Troopers was released 25 years ago on this very day and thought about watching it later.

Wait I forget when did you find the first larva?

Larvae.

The first larvae.

The first moment was . . . well first I must tell you that we had been really busy for two weekends in a row so I didn't have time to do my usual sweeping and dusting and vacuuming she said.

The wedding in Maine.

Yes that weekend.

That was a nice weekend.

It was a very nice weekend yes. We saw your friend at the bar randomly and he seemed to be doing poorly but also fine.

That is about as good as you can ask for.

Well when I got around to cleaning I was sweeping upstairs in the bedroom and I swept up a pile of dust bunnies into what's the thing you sweep into? The bin? You know what I'm talking about? The part that you sweep it into?

The tray?

The tray. Not that. I don't think that's the word. Then I noticed a couple of little brown things moving around and looked closer. I thought nothing of it and killed them. Then I swept in the bathroom and the same thing happened. I saw a couple of gray brown guys moving. Then I cleared the whole house but in the back of my head I thought hm that's weird I don't usually sweep up bugs. The next day I figured I'd look into things more.

After sleeping on it?

After sleeping on it. So I opened the closet and inspected the top row of clothes. There was one of the little guys. Right there. In the back row where the clothes we never wear hang. All your shirts that don't fit you anymore.

Come on.

Sorry but you know what I mean. Tucked back in there was a blazer you wore at __'s wedding all those years ago. I noticed it had some yellowish wormy looking guys on it. It was completely eaten through with so many holes. You sang a song at their wedding. I just thought of that. So I started pulling clothes out. I had you go get a trash bag and I put it all in the trash bag. You know all of this why are you asking me?

I forgot what happened. I wasn't feeling well. I don't know why but I forgot he said. I'm not feeling very well now if I'm honest.

There was a hammering in the near distance. Chunk chunk chunk. They were used to the sound of the shooting range up the road so it was only momentarily distracting.

It's just the gun people she said.

What was motivating this level of alertness on your part do you suppose he asked.

I have a very deep fear of infestations she said. Anything that involves an infestation makes me incredibly anxious. Staying in hotels makes me anxious about bed bugs. I guess that's probably the best example. It probably goes to a control thing. Where I worry that there's going to be a problem that I can't control. And uh this probably also has to do with control too because I'm OCD about things. There are certain things with cleanliness where I'm very compulsive.

I don't really have that problem haha. I guess that's not funny I'm sorry.

You're compulsive but you have a different type of compulsion haha.

A truck was groaning outside and there was a thud on the stoop.

Did you order something he asked.

Yes she said.

What did you order?

Nothing she said.

In particular the thing that really bothers me about it is that these specific bugs can ruin clothing and rugs and upholstery and even furniture she said. My home is my heart. It's the only place in the world I feel calm all the time. And like protected from the cruel world. And happy. And in my place. So the idea of not being able to control something that's ruining my sense of order and safety in this world truly upsets me on a very existential level. I want to tell you something I've been reflecting on . . .

Please do.

Well it's my deep connection to capitalism.

How so?

It upsets me that I want to have nice things! That's kind of weird to care about. That you have nice things without holes in them. Maybe it's internalized misogyny. Keeping a nice home. I can't really verbalize it but I know it's in there. Inside of me. So contributing to that . . .

What's the worst case scenario do you think for the larvae in terms of encroaching on your controlled space?

That they never go away! Obviously. That no matter what I do they never go away. Another reason it's upsetting is what if one crawls in my ear when I sleep?

Sometimes I wake up in the middle of the night and I have to stretch my jaw open because I've been clenching it so tightly dreaming about everything I've ever done wrong he said.

I have to stretch my tongue all the time when I'm driving. Why are you saying that do you think a bug might crawl into it?

Do birds have tongues he said.

I think so.

That fucks me up for some reason but I guess it makes sense he said.

Yeah so bugs getting into my mouth is one concern of mine he said. I don't mind swallowing a small bug he said. Often when I go for a run some little kind of flying guy will bungle into my open gasping mouth and it's always a tough call whether to gag it out or to just say fuck it and swallow. It depends on how much moisture you have and at what point in the run it happens. If you've been sweating for forty minutes you don't have saliva to spare. But I don't like the idea of swallowing a bug that might not die instantly on the journey you know? Like an action hero bug or a spaceship type of thing where they navigate my esophagus and emerge covered in my slime and want revenge.

That could happen. You probably do eat spiders when you sleep. I'm not as afraid of spiders because their populations tend to be like normal. I just don't like things that can infest. It's about control but I think it's normal to not want that.

I'd say that's very normal.

Remember when we ate all those crickets in Mexico she said.

They were surprisingly good!

They were pretty good but I think it was like the whole thing of it. Being somewhere else and not wanting to not try things she said.

We stayed in a convent they'd turned into a douchey hotel.

And the people from Miami!

Oh god. The hotel was nice though.

It really was. I was going to say one of the most horrifying stories for me was some news thing I read from Australia she said. I think it was Australia. The whole town became mouse-infested and people just couldn't get them out of their houses. They washed their blankets and when they took them out they found dead mice in there spun and heated in the water and folded into the fabric. They couldn't get rid of these mice. Things like that make my skin crawl. I hate the idea of things I can't get away from or clean up or control. It's also the fear of the unknown. I like to know exactly what's going to happen. I don't want to wait and see I want to do something now and know. Hold on is somebody out there at the window?

No but let me look he said. No there isn't.

Maybe it's the people shooting. The shooting people.

It's just the trash bins blowing over. I'll take them in later he said.

Mice are like the last of their problems in Australia he said. They have like ten foot spiders and lizards that are basically monsters from space.

It might not have been Australia she said. It was some place in… I read an article about it a couple years ago. It keeps me up at night sometimes. What if that happens here? The woman who lived in this house before us was terrified of spiders did you know that?

No why would I know that?

You never listen to me. Our neighbors told us. To the point she had all the bushes pulled up because they had spiders in them. Big giant draping webs like you'd put up for Halloween but they were real. She'd have to call the neighbors for help killing the spiders because she was so frightened. They'd come over with whatever poison they had under the sink. We still have a fair amount of spiders here though. It seems like the spiders won that battle.

I know and I hate them he said. I don't love a spider! Maybe we can sort of pit them against the larvae here? A kind of Godzilla versus Mothra type situation? Let nature take its course.

I don't love them either but more so I don't like it when I see twenty of something. When they're really good at producing eggs and multiplying that makes me feel crazy.

Did you see Heidi Klum's costume?

Why? Oh because of the theme we're working inside of.

Yeah.

Well she . . .

I don't love it but it's more just funny. How do you spell Scarlet Johanson?

Scarlett Johansson. Two t's two s's.

So afterwards she took off the worm body and emerged like a chrysalis in another photo I saw. A vile monster blossoming into a run of the mill hot lady.

These hot bitches.

I know but she still had the face mask of the worm on. Like strips of raw bacon wrapped around her pretty face. It was like that movie you fell asleep for . . .

You have to narrow it down there.

Under the Skin with Scarlet . . . t Johans . . . son.

You would of course love that one.

It wasn't like that.

No?

Ok it was like that but not like that. It's just such a quiet and slow movie. I'm never going to stop thinking about it. She's this alien that is part scout and part hunter that scoops up dumb shits along the side of the road whose fatal flaw is being horny for Scarlett Johansson and needing a ride somewhere which are two universal human experiences.

I forget what she did with them.

Well we don't know. Ate them I guess. Close enough to that. Like we do with pigs and cows I guess but the way the harvesting was rendered obliquely and stylized and sort of withheld in the film was so much scarier and imaginative than something gory would've been. Something where you actually could see what was happening. It's much worse to not fully understand how someone or something is dying.

Wait why are you asking me all of this she said. About the larvae I mean she said.

Do you trust me he said.

I don't think so.

You don't trust me?

I don't know.

He crawled into bed first that night which was the incorrect order of things and wrestled to drift off with the sound of the vacuum whirring and devouring downstairs. He listened in his memory to Low singing When I Go Deaf. Gradually at first and then suddenly the pills started to shave off the edges of everything like when you pinch in the borders of a photo on your phone and his body downshifted into its initial descent and the last thing he remembered was hearing a rustling in the closet. He thought of a nervous dog turning around and turning around before settling onto a cushion in its crate.

Did you ever watch a horror movie where it's like a captivity scenario and they eventually show the fucked up basement with the green lighting where the characters are being kept in iron cages starving and shitting and bleeding and weeping all over themselves and the main girl the prettiest one they could hire for the role runs through and she's bouncing off the walls in her tank top as she flees like holy fuck holy fuck and think I wouldn't stand for that type of shit. Unlike these poor sons of bitches who made a bad decision you might think this is something I would not have let happen. I would figure out a way to forestall this evil done upon my person is what you might think. If not to ultimately abscond to freedom and have my vengeance if it's fairly proved impossible then at least to puncture your jugular on the screw of the cage's fitting out of spite. Fasten your own hair ripped from a shredded scalp into a noose.

That was one kind of dream.

I've been worried about my friend who's been on the verge of self-induced oblivion for many years and thought I reacted poorly to his latest cry for help and it took me weeks to realize that it wasn't that I did not care anymore but rather that I had cared for so long and so deeply that it formed a blockage in my chest and my tolerance equilibrium was thrown off its axis. How after you cry for an hour or two over a loss and then are like alright cut the shit. This caring isn't going to thwart a single thing. Not one single thing will change due to this caring.

He stirred a few hours later and she had finally come to bed and the house was silent save for a faint panting. He stretched out his jaw and thought nothing of what might crawl inside of it.

The next day he called around to find a guy and the first one to say yes seemed decent enough so then here he arrived with his little canister of bullshit spraying it under the baseboards and everywhere. I've seen a lot worse the guy said misting this and that like you'd water plants but doing the opposite now not nourishing the living but sickening them instead.

As it happened the guy had recently purchased a home near where his family usually stayed in Maine and so they talked about that for a while trading references to obvious landmarks back and forth that neither seemed to recognize.

Near the church there? I don't think we've ever been there.

Oh weird it's right there.

It was unclear to him whether or not you're supposed to tip a pest control guy and all he had was a baggie full of roughly twelve dollars in quarters but weighing his options and not wanting to seem cheap he poured them into this other man's cupped hands feeling like God's Unique Asshole and thinking it would have been better to have just stiffed him instead of doing anything like this.

When the pest man left he looked out the window at his truck and saw some political bumper stickers that soured his impression of the entire ordeal even further. My affable demeanor and ability to display interpersonal kindness is hiding something much worse underneath one read. Man's inhumanity to man is good actually said a second. A third was a Pearl Jam sticker and that was one kind of a toss up on what it indicated.

You should also ask me about the checking on how long it takes me to leave the house she said.

What are you talking about?

That's a whole other thing related to how the bugs molest me. You don't think they're related? The longer we're not going to be home the longer it takes me to leave the house. My worries about the house still being here in the same way we left it is a multiplicative relationship.

What does multiplicative mean?

What was that she said tracing an invisible flight pattern across the expansive canopy of the living room sky. Was that a moth?

I didn't see it? I think you're still just wound up he said.

Ah I know how that sounds he said. I'm sorry.

Multiplicative means like multiplied a few times as much she said. For every day we won't be here it takes ten minutes to check the house to make sure it's gonna be just like this when we come back. Like the amount of times I check the stove. If we're going out for an hour I'll check it once. Two days I'll check it three times. Longer than that I'll take a picture and check it ten times.

But the stove is never hot. It doesn't turn on when we aren't looking. It has never turned on by itself. A stove does not have agency baby.

That doesn't matter. That doesn't matter at all.

But it does baby.

I'm sorry before all of this you were trying to tell me about your therapy session she said. How did it go?

It was fine.

Come on.

Well if you really care I talked about some dreams I've been having. She told me that she wasn't a Jungian but that we could explore them a bit if I liked and I spent the rest of the time worrying about if she pronounced Jungian right.

Did she? Wait what was that? Outside?

Nothing. I don't know. How would I know?

He went to look and there was a figure knocking on the door and the sound of children murmuring.

Is trick or treating tonight?

Oh shit she said.

But it's not Halloween yet.

That's how they're doing it this year she said. As a precaution.

He opened the door to greet Spider-Man and his friend the fairy princess. Hold on kids he said. Hold on just a minute now we're gonna get you something to eat.

Give us the treats they said.

So did she pronounce it right she asked after the coast was clear.

271

I honestly don't remember. I forgot to look it up. I used to know that. I used to know so many things.

Yunyun?

Yunyun.

That takes me back to working in kitchens she said. Coming up behind someone with a hot pan and saying yanyo she said and they both laughed.

Yanyo.

A little sing-song cadence.

Yanyo.

So I told the therapist the one dream I have about being at the top of a towering edifice of one kind or another and being constantly aware of the hungry chasm below the entire time just never not aware for one second of the distance to the ground and increasingly in my fevered climbing how much longer the plummeting would take to be completed and the fear every moment that someone most often you would trip off the ledge and I'd be left to grasp onto your hand and pull you back to safety but I just cannot do it he said.

Did your therapist have an idea what that might mean?

Yes but I don't want to say it out loud.

Wait what the fuck was that?

Just the neighbors. Their dog. Maybe the dog. The shooting people. The dogs and the shooting people and the kids in costumes he said.

Then there was the one about returning to my high school football team after being away for a year or two and it being a whole thing among the team that I was there no one entirely sure what to make of me and then after all of the build up I can't find my helmet he said. Wait what are you doing are you looking for bugs right now?

I'm still listening.

I'm not going to talk to you while you're bug hunting.

I'm sorry baby.

Baby I am also sorry. Did you see __'s post about considering getting divorced so they could afford to have their baby? How their insurance was fucking with them so much that they couldn't see any other way through it.

No. No come on.

What if we left the bugs be for now he said. There's supposed to be an extraordinary moon out tonight do you want to go look at it?

Is your therapist attractive she said.

What.

Is she hot?

No. God no. Can you imagine? What a nightmare that would be.

Do you want to fuck her though? Even though she's not hot?

I don't know. No.

She went off into the basement to look for a tool she was sure would be helpful in her pursuit of cleanliness and he made a good faith effort to scan the edges of the living room for larvae but couldn't see any. He looked at his phone again and saw a video of Customs and Border Patrol agents shooting rubber bullets at migrants near the Rio Grande in El Paso and the people were all running away plunging back into the river because water even dangerous water is more forgiving than soldiers although there's always a tipping point in that equation. The problem is when you are fleeing for your life you have to do the math so quickly.

All they wanted were some nice things he thought.

He went outside and sat on a chair in the yard when a bird alighted on the ground in front of him. It had been warmer than it should have rightfully been all week and the air felt like it had blown in from the wrong direction. The gnats and mosquitos were buzzing around dizzied and confused and unaware that they didn't belong here. None of the correct things were alive at this particular juncture. None of these creatures were supposed to be alive.

He was waiting for the bird to speak or to do anything but sit there dumbly staring but it of course did not say anything it wasn't that kind of bird. He had this stupid idea that he could reach out and grab it by the neck. He knew it was impossible but he thought it anyway. That he was fast enough to do that.

Illustrations

174   Image from Abel Aubert Du Petit-Thouars. *Voyage autour du monde sur la frégate la Vénus Zoologie: mammifères, oiseaux, reptiles, et poisons.* Paris: Gide et J. Baudry, 1846 [atlas]-1855 [text].

184   Image from Johan Ludwig Gerhard Krefft. *The snakes of Australia: an illustrated and descriptive catalogue of all the known species.* Sydney: Government Printer, 1869.

197   Image from Thomas Horsfield. *Zoological researches in Java, and the neighbouring islands.* London: Printed for Kingsbury, Parbury, & Allen, 1824.

201   Image from Christian Heinrich Pander. *Die vergleichende Osteologie.* Bonn: 1821–1838.

207   Image from Jules-Sébastien-César Dumont d'Urville. *Voyage au pole sud et dans l'Océanie sur les corvettes.* Paris: Gide et. J Baudry, Éditeurs 1842–1854.

215   Image from Thomas Horsfield. *Zoological researches in Java, and the neighbouring islands.* London: Printed for Kingsbury, Parbury, & Allen, 1824.

224   Image from Jonathan Couch. *A history of the fishes of the British islands.* London, Groombridge: 1868–1869.

227   Image from George Robert Gray and John Edward Gray. *Lepidoptera of Nepal.* London: Longman, Brown, Green, and Longmans, 1846.

235   Image from Philipp Franz von Siebold. *Fauna japonica.* Lugduni Batavorum: Apud Auctorem, 1833–1850.

244   Image from Elizabeth Gould, John Gould, and Edward Lear. *The Birds of Europe.* London: R. and J.E. Taylor, pub. by author, 1837.

All illustrations sourced from the Biodiversity Heritage Library photostream, https://www.flickr.com/people/biodivlibrary/.